Smith's
MONTHLY

Every Month Original Novels, Stories, and Articles

USA Today Bestselling Writer
Dean Wesley Smith

TABLE OF CONTENTS

Smith's Monthly Issue #28

The Writings and Opinions of
Dean Wesley Smith

Introduction
A FIRST NOVEL

For the longest time, when people would ask me if I would ever reprint my first published novel, *Laying the Music to Rest*, I always said no. It wasn't because I was embarrassed by it. Far from that, actually.

And yes, in the almost thirty years since I wrote this book, I have become a far better storyteller and I could go on about the things I would do differently in this book if I told it now. But I won't. I promise.

In fact, I'm not going to change a word from the published version that came out in paperback in 1989 from Warner Questar Books.

Not one word, other than fixing some typos that were in the published version.

The book is a good book and I am still proud of it. Especially as a first novel.

Why I didn't want to bring the book back into print is actually because of the names and the ideas in it. You will see as you read this book over the months some echoes of my writing now.

For example, I set this novel in Idaho, at Lake Roosevelt, the lake with the old mining town under it. In my Thunder Mountain series, which is far better researched than this book ever was, the entire series rotates around the same area.

In fact, I took some pretty good liberties with the area around the lake in this book. I had only visited the lake once when I wrote this, and considering how remote the area was and how little is known about that area, I forgive myself for the mistakes.

I got the area in this book a lot closer to fact than Zane Gray did in his novel *Thunder Mountain* about the same area.

So in this first novel, you can get a hint of the writing I would do much later in my writing life.

Also, the main character is named "Doc" in this book. I also, two decades later, created a Doc Hill as a major character in a thriller I wrote and he still plays a part in my Cold Poker Gang series of mysteries at times. Not the same Doc at all.

Thanks for the Support

Dean Wesley Smith

One other point of connection to my future writing. I set the opening of this in the Garden Lounge in Boise. The Garden Lounge plays an important part in all my jukebox stories. Not the same Garden Lounge either.

So as I looked back at this book, I saw all kinds of hints of my future writing in my first novel. There are other hints later in the book that connect to my Seeders Universe novels, but actually are not the same either.

So this book that starts its serialization here is a great glimpse of my future writing.

And that brings me to the reason I am finally republishing this novel after all these years.

By the time I get done serializing it in these pages and then WMG publishes the book, it will be almost exactly thirty years since I wrote it.

Not many writers are still active and publishing novels thirty years after their first novel was written. (I wrote it in 1987, sold it in May of 1988 and it was published in 1989.)

I am very proud of having published almost 150 novels now and survived for thirty years making my living in publishing. So I wanted to celebrate that point by bringing my first published (not written) novel back into print in my own magazine.

And not just the first issue of my own magazine, but the 28th issue through the 36th or so issue.

I just find it wonderful that I wrote *Laying the Music to Rest* and put in so many seeds of ideas that would be explored in the future. And now I am still going strong.

So I am proud of myself. And I wanted to get the novel that started it all back into print just before the 30th anniversary of my writing it.

I hope you enjoy the read.

—Dean Wesley Smith
January 12, 2016

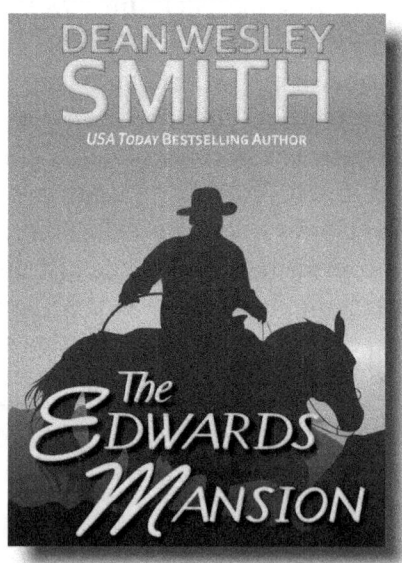

Two Thunder Mountain Novels
Available at your favorite booksellers.

Coming Next Issue in *Smith's Monthly*

DEAD HAND

A Cold Poker Gang Mystery

When you're a superhero, you don't often notice pink shoes.

Poker Boy is usually far too busy saving the world from evil, saving dogs from sure death, or playing professional poker, his day job that pays the bills of being a superhero.

But when Poker Boy sees the pink shoes at the entrance to the Silicon Suckers city, he knows Super Keno is in big trouble.

PINK SHOES AND HOT CHOCOLATE
A Poker Boy Story

ONE

WHEN YOU'RE A superhero, you don't often notice pink women's shoes. I'm usually far too busy saving the world from evil, saving dogs from sure death, or playing professional poker, my day job that pays the bills of being a superhero. Pink shoes rarely come into the picture. In fact, I have no memory of ever thinking about pink shoes before.

Yet there sat a pair of bright pink dress shoes with very long heels on the small pile of brown sand six miles outside of Las Vegas.

The wind was blowing through the sagebrush and rocks and I was having trouble keeping my black, Fedora-like poker hat on my head. The hat was part of my superhero costume, along with my black leather jacket. With the hat and jacket on and a casino nearby, I had more powers than I have had time to explore. Sometimes my powers even surprise me.

But out in the desert, with the wind threatening to take my hat and make me chase it like a playful dog through the rocks, I didn't feel very powerful. And the pair of women's pink shoes sitting on the mound didn't help the issue.

Around me, the very early morning sun was heating up the desert to the point that shortly it would be far too warm for me to wear my black leather jacket even with a wind. The heat was the reason I had headed out of town at five in the morning. I never saw five in the morning normally, except from the night side. Getting up at this frightful hour showed how much I cared about this case. It had taken me only an hour to find the shoes, since I had a hunch exactly where to look.

The pink shoes belonged to Carol Savage, a thin, athletic Keno runner at the Atlantis Hotel and Casino. Carol stood two inches taller than my six-foot height and she was much, much thinner. Not that I'm fat. I'm not. Carol is just thin.

Carol had a smile that could light up a room and her dark green eyes seemed to laugh at everything. I figured she had to have a great life attitude, being a Keno runner. The old joke around the poker world was that Keno was for gamblers who had lost the will to live. Carol radiated life like the sun gave off light. She was a joy to be around, always.

Bernice, the God of Keno, hated that old joke, but of all the Gambling Gods, she was the lowest ranked and only had one superhero like me working under her. That was Carol, also known as SK (Super Keno) to the rest of the Gambling Gods and all the superheroes who worked for them.

Everyone liked SK; Bernice we could all do without.

When Carol went missing, I got the first call to help find her. Every one of the Gambling Gods seemed to know that she and I had been an item five or six years back, working a couple of cases together. That was before I met Front Desk Girl.

I am known as Poker Boy, one of a dozen poker superheroes working under Stan, the God of Poker.

And, of course, we all worked under Laverne, Lady Luck herself. And when Laverne asked Stan to have me search for Carol, what was I going to say? Hell, you don't turn down Lady Luck if you ever wanted to win another hand of cards.

With one hand I held my hat on my head and with the other I picked up Carol's pink shoes and studied them. Nothing unusual. She had simply kicked them off and put them on the sand.

I had seen no sign of Carol's car along the road, or any car parked close by, so either she had hidden it in the desert somewhere or someone had dropped her off here.

I placed the pink shoes back exactly where Carol had left them and studied the flat desert around me, squinting my eyes and trying to draw on what superpowers I had remaining this far from a casino. It wasn't much, I do have to admit, like a car trying to run on three of six cylinders. I sputtered a lot, but finally found what I was looking for.

There, in plain sight, yet hidden so any normal mortal would never see it, was the opening to the Silicon Suckers city. I had no idea why Carol hadn't used the main entrance under the Hilton Billboard on Highway 95, but she must have had her reasons. I knew the desert was scattered with entrances to the Silicon Sucker's city, but I had only found one other besides the main entrance and this one.

Silicon Suckers were a race of intelligent creatures that had lived on Earth

Now Available
from all your favorite booksellers
in trade paper and electronic editions.

far, far longer than mankind. They were secretive and shy at best, and almost impossible to see if they didn't want to be seen. They inhabited the major deserts of the world, living in cities underground.

Legends of aliens visiting Earth had come about from sightings of Silicon Suckers. They were commonly called The Grays by UFO nuts. They had large heads, large eyes, no chins, and flat ears. Their arms and legs were thinner than Carol's and they seldom wore clothes. Even without clothes, I couldn't tell the difference between a female and a male Silicon Sucker, although I was told that the difference was clear if you knew what you were looking for.

With humans I knew. Not a clue with Silicon Suckers and I had no great desire to look.

The Silicon Suckers were a highly ritualized race, and the best way to get on their bad side was to violate one of their customs. Wearing shoes in their city was a major violation. Not bringing them a gift they would like when visiting was another. I had a small thermos of hot chocolate in my jacket pocket as my gift to them. Hot chocolate, for some reason or another, was a major delicacy for them. A thermos-full would be shared by the drop among thousands.

I once watched a Silicon Sucker put a drop of hot chocolate on his snake-like tongue and then just stand there, huge eyes closed, swaying back and forth humming something that sounded a lot like our National Anthem played very, very slowly.

Whatever the Silicon Sucker experienced with the hot chocolate was clearly something I could only imagine, since I didn't drink and have never taken drugs of any kind.

I just hoped Carol had known enough about the Suckers to bring them something good. I had a hunch, though, she had done something very, very wrong, since after three days missing, her shoes were still here.

Just in case I needed to buy her way out, I had two other thermoses full of hot chocolate in pockets inside my coat.

I took a deep breath, kicked off my old Nike tennis shoes and left them beside Carol's pink shoes, then headed for the opening between the two rocks. I had been inside the Silicon Sucker's city near Las Vegas three times over my years as a superhero, and it always made me uncomfortable and itchy. The last time I had been trying to save the life of an old college girlfriend who had been given new breast implants made from the sand of a sacred Silicon Suckers burial site.

The Suckers wanted their dead ancestors back; my old girlfriend wasn't willing to give them back, no matter how much I pleaded or offered to pay for another operation. She was found dead a month later. I seldom like to think how she died, since the myth about alien probes have a basis in the Silicon Suckers' belief that the only way inside a human body is through the anus.

Those were very large breasts she had. It had to have been painful.

TWO

I HAD NO IDEA what case Carol had been working for the Gambling Gods to take her to a Silicon Suckers city.

But Stan had told me to look here first, and I had found her shoes at the second entrance I checked.

I stopped at the entrance to the city, bowed once exactly as prescribed for any visitor to the city, and then stepped through the slight magic spell that hid the entrance from normal humans.

Inside the dry, brown cave, two Silicon Suckers bowed in return and then indicated I should follow them.

My nose was assaulted by the smell of sand and an intense dryness to the air. My skin felt suddenly tight as if the air was trying to suck every ounce of moisture from my body.

Actually, it was.

They led me down toward the city in what looked like nothing more than a cave carved out of the desert sand and rock. It was lit faintly by soft lights hidden along the ceiling. The more we walked, the raspier my throat felt. It had happened every time to me, but no water was allowed in their cities, so I hadn't dared bring anything to help with the dryness and intense thirst that would soon hit me.

And drinking any of the hot chocolate I had with me while in their city was considered a terminal offense.

I worried a lot about Carol being able to survive three days without water in this environment. I know I would have a hard time.

It wasn't until we had walked downward for almost a half hour that we finally emerged into the vast central chamber of the Silicon Suckers city.

The first time I had seen the massive city with the teeming thousands of Suckers moving about their daily lives, I had been stunned. This time was no different.

Towers of sand-colored round buildings shot from the cavern floor at least thirty stories into the air, elevated walkways spanned the open spaces between the buildings, and the entire cavern hummed with a distant ocean sound that I

had been told was nothing more than the sound of a lot of Silicon Suckers moving around at once.

The cavern was lit by an intense, sun-like light, right in the middle and thousands of other lights on the buildings and along the wide streets. No carriages or any type of transportation moved inside the city. Silicon Suckers walked everywhere they went.

And the huge chamber felt even drier than the tunnels, if that was possible. It smelled of lightly burned wood, and I found myself blinking a lot more than normal to keep some hint of moisture in my eyes.

Thousands and thousands of openings went into the dirt all the way around the cavern. We had come out of one such opening about twenty stories in the air, and immediately started down a fairly wide path along the wall.

There was no guardrail on the edge of the path, so I stayed to the inside, hugging the wall. I might be a superhero in the gambling world, but I was fairly certain that none of my superpowers included flying. Flying just didn't seem to be of much use at a poker table.

Without ever asking me what I wanted or who I wanted to see, my two guides led me down to the ground level of the city, then into a building that had to be twenty stories tall and was fairly close to the center of the city. I couldn't tell one tall, brown tower from another, but for some reason this one felt special to me.

Inside they led me into another tunnel that continued down for another two or three stories, finally opening into a large chamber with four Silicon Suckers sitting cross-legged in the middle of the floor in a circle.

Carol sat cross-legged with them, nodding at something.

She glanced up and saw me, then burst into a huge smile that must have hurt her extremely chapped and dry lips.

"Poker Boy," she said without standing. "Thanks for coming."

"Laverne sent me," I said, moving toward the circle.

"I know," Carol said, a twinkle in her eyes.

I had no idea how she could know that. But asking at that moment just seemed very, very wrong.

THREE

ONE OF MY guides indicated that I should sit in the open spot in the circle beside Carol facing the four Silicon Suckers.

Even though I wanted to hug or even lightly touch Carol to tell her I was glad to see her, I knew something as simple as a touch between humans in a Silicon Sucker city would a very bad breach of protocol, and since I had no idea what was going on or what part I was to play, I was very careful to not sit too near Carol.

After taking my position, I reached into my front pocket and pulled out a thermos of hot chocolate.

In my best Silicon Sucker click and wheep and stutter, I said, "A gift to thank you for the honor of visiting your wonderful city."

At least I hope that was what I said.

I set the thermos down and placed my hands in my lap, bowing my head in just the right manner to show respect.

"We accept your wonderful gift to our people. Welcome again, Poker Boy. You are always an honored member of our city."

The Silicon Sucker who spoke didn't move his tiny lips and I wasn't sure if I heard his words with my ears or inside my head. Didn't matter, at least he spoke in English and I didn't have to attempt his language any more.

I nodded my thank you, as prescribed, but said nothing more.

"May we resume our discussions?" Carol asked, her words sounding hoarse from so much exposure to the dry air.

I had no idea how, if she had been down here for three days, she was even managing to sit and talk. Her strength stunned me, but clearly it was wearing on her. Even a superhero like her had limits.

The Silicon Sucker on the right nodded and in the middle of the circle, floating in the air, a map appeared, shimmering and see-through.

It took me a moment to realize exactly what I was looking at. The Silicon Suckers city was colored in gold on the map, their sacred burial grounds in gold, as well as large acres of other ground I had no idea what they used it for. Highway 95 on one side marked one border and the edge of the city of Las Vegas was a black area on the map.

It seemed that a tiny area just off Highway 95 was in question, as it was blinking between gold and black. When I realized the scale of the map, that tiny area suddenly became larger than a hundred acres.

"I am sure we can come to a fair exchange for the land in question," Carol said, nodding her respect as she spoke. "Poker Boy has brought the first of our many payments to you."

Carol nodded to me and I stared at her for a moment, wondering for a second just exactly what she was talking about. Then I remembered the two other thermoses of hot chocolate I had inside my coat.

I took out one and placed it carefully beside the first, bowing with respect as I did, then placed the third beside the other two.

I had no idea what to say at such a moment, and as I had learned over the years in both poker and doing superhero deeds, if you aren't sure exactly what to say, say nothing.

But damned if I didn't want to ask Carol how she knew I would bring those extra two thermoses with me.

Carol bowed slightly to the Silicon Suckers. "Only the first of many payments to come in exchange for the use of your very valuable land."

"May we understand, please, that your people will bring us every full moon cycle, ten such containers of the precious fluid?"

Carol nodded. "That is my understanding, yes."

I almost snorted, which would have been a huge breach in protocol and more than likely an insult in the Silicon Suckers language. I couldn't believe that Carol was trading what looked like a good one hundred acres of land near Highway 95 for basically ten large mugs of hot chocolate per month. I knew land prices were down, but that was ridiculous.

FOUR

"IT IS AGREED," the Silicon Sucker said. The parcel on the map that had been going between gold and black turned black and stayed black.

"It is agreed," Carol said.

The map vanished and the four Silicon Suckers stood and turned away, moving toward an opening in the brown sand wall.

Carol struggled to her feet and stood, clearly exhausted and dehydrated. She needed to get to the hospital and get there quickly, but there was no way I could dare touch her to help her until we cleared that entrance a good fifty stories over our heads.

Our two guides appeared and nodded that we should follow them. I stepped in behind Carol and we headed upward through what I thought was the same tunnel we had come down.

For the first hundred or so steps, Carol staggered, and I was afraid she was going to fall, then she seemed to gain some inner strength and her back straightened, her head came up, and she looked straight ahead as if walking the floor selling Keno tickets.

She was one strong lady.

Back at the surface, we both bowed to our guides and stepped through into the extreme temperatures of the desert in the middle of the afternoon. It had to be well over one hundred and the dry wind hit us both like a hammer.

Carol walked ten steps and then went down, face-first, right on her pink shoes.

The hot wind battered at my hat as I knelt beside her. She was out completely, and from the looks of her in the light, she was on the verge of dying from dehydration.

I snapped open my cell phone and called 911, telling them where along the highway to have an ambulance meet me, then I called my girlfriend and sidekick, Patty Ledgerwood, a.k.a. Front Desk Girl, and told her to find Stan and tell him

I was coming in with SK and to get our people at the hospital ready.

I carried the thin Keno-runner super-hero to my rental car and laid her out on the back seat. She weighed almost nothing and that scared me a lot. She couldn't die for a piece of property. That just seemed too stupid. I had almost died a number of times trying to rescue a person, but never for a real estate sale, especially in a bad market.

FIVE

I MET THE ambulance at the corner I had indicated, and they worked on her for a good fifteen minutes, getting fluid into her system and checking her vitals before loading her into the ambulance and rushing to the hospital, lights and sirens blaring, with me right on their tail.

By the time I had parked and gotten into the emergency room, she was out of sight. Patty, Stan, and Bernice were all in the waiting room looking worried.

"Good job getting her out of there," Stan said. "Did she get the deal done?"

"She did," I said, staring at Stan, surprised. "You knew what she was doing in there?"

"Not until Bernice told me," Stan said, clearly disgusted, "after you had left."

I stared at Bernice, a short stubby little god that I didn't much like and had even less respect for. "You want to tell me why you risked Carol's life on a property deal with the Silicon Suckers?"

"Huge new Bingo and Keno parlor is planned for that ground along with a large retirement home. The county wouldn't agree, of course, since the gods blocked building on any of the Silicon Suckers' ground. It was the only way to get the approval."

"And that was worth Carol's life?"

"Of course not," Bernice snapped. "That's why we sent you in to rescue her. The negotiations were only supposed to take a day and we didn't expect her to succeed. We knew things had gone wrong when she hadn't come out in two days."

I gave the short little Keno God my most intense poker stare until she turned away and started pacing.

Stan patted me on the shoulder. "Laverne's in there with her. Carol will make it."

Patty slipped her hand into mine and I could feel the calming influence she had over me. Her super powers concerned making people happy, among other things, and she could calm me down with a touch.

She pulled me over to a row of black, plastic chairs along one wall and we sat down. She handed me a bottle of water and I downed it quickly. Never had water tasted so good.

She handed me another after I finished the first bottle, then said, "So, you want to tell me what happened to your shoes?"

I glanced down at my feet and the very dirty white socks I still wore. "They are beside Carol's pink dress shoes, at the entrance to the Silicon Suckers city. Can't wear shoes down there."

Over the next half hour I told her and Stan and Bernice exactly what had happened and what Carol had managed to do, including the long walk back to the surface on her own.

Just as I finished, Laverne, Lady Luck herself, walked out of the back of the emergency room area and nodded. "She's going to make it. She's asleep and can have visitors tomorrow."

"Oh, thank you," Bernice said, slumping in her chair.

"Nice job once again, Poker Boy," Laverne said. I could only smile. When Lady Luck herself thanked you, there just wasn't much to say.

Patty squeezed my hand.

"We have to talk," Laverne said, staring at Bernice.

They both vanished.

"Good job, kid," Stan said and vanished as well.

Patty helped me to my feet and we headed toward the door. Outside, in the heat, I really noticed that I didn't have shoes as I moved from one shaded area to the next across the hot pavement.

As we got settled in my car, Patty turned to me. "I still don't get the hot chocolate part of all this."

"Think drugs," I said. "Hot chocolate is their most valuable drug."

"So how did you know to take extra hot chocolate, and how did Carol know you were bringing it?"

"You want my guess?" I asked and Front Desk Girl nodded.

"Carol knew that I would be the one the gods picked to try to find her, since I knew her and had dealings in the past with the Silicon Suckers."

"Got that," Patty said.

"And after being down there for three days, Carol knew I would bring the only real thing of value to a Silicon Sucker to buy her freedom, so she used it as a lure in the purchase instead of a bribe for her release."

"That could have gone so very wrong," Front Desk Girl said.

"Carol knows me, and clearly knew who she was negotiating with. Something must have happened to force her to stay that long and take such a huge risk. We won't know exactly what went wrong until tomorrow."

Front Desk Girl shook her head. "Hot chocolate as a drug. Who would have thought?"

"I can understand that on a cold winter night in front of a crackling fire."

"I thought I was your drug of choice," she said, laughing and rubbing her hand along my leg, sending happy feelings throughout my tired body.

"Oh, you are, you are."

She looked at me with a smile that could melt any angry customer standing at a front desk, let alone a tired poker player.

"How about we go back to my place and I'll get you a couple more bottles of water and help you scrub off some of that sand and dirt in a nice cool shower?"

"Perfect," I said. "But first, can we go get my shoes and Carol's shoes from the desert?"

"Sure, but why? I've seen your shoes and they aren't worth the gas out there."

"Not for mine, for Carol's shoes," I said. "In all my years of being a superhero, I've never rescued pink shoes before."

Patty laughed. "I guess there's a first time for everything."

Can't Get Enough of Poker Boy?
These stories and more are available at your favorite booksellers.

Now Available
from all your favorite booksellers
in trade paper and electronic editions.

Dean Wesley **Smith**

USA Today Bestselling Writer

Dinner
on a
Flying Saucer

Sometimes, tellin' your
wife the truth
ain't such a fine idea.

Sometimes, when a fella gets to help out with fightin' a war between two alien races, it's just not such a good idea to tell your wife.

Sometimes the truth just isn't good enough.

DINNER ON A FLYING SAUCER

ETHEL WAS LOOKIN' at me like a skunk done crawled up my ass and was making a nest. I suppose I couldn't really be blamin' her. I figure that havin' dinner on a flyin' saucer would be a hard lump to swallow whole, especially when I smelled of whiskey and had lipstick-lookin' red marks all over my coveralls.

And, to boot, it was three in the mornin'.

Ethel stood there in the front door of the double-wide that I had bought and paid for with the sweat and hard work from my own bare hands like she owned the thing, leavin' me stuck on the second step halfway up to the porch like a dog after he rolled in the mud. She was makin' sure I didn't have a thought of goin' inside past her, even though it was cold and kinda real damp out.

Behind her, the light from the kitchen was showin' through her bathrobe and nightgown, outlinin' things that Ethel should *never* let be seen.

Now no disrespect to my wife, but Ethel is a big woman, taller by a pretty fine lick than my five-foot height. She never was much of a sight to look at at three in the morning, and this morning was no great exception to the rule. She had them there big curlers in her hair that jabbed me every darned time I rolled over in bed. She had on her flannel robe over her nightgown, and her favorite slippers with the pink furballs on the toes. Right at that moment her face was all screwed up like she was about to spit, and she had my shotgun cradled under her tits just like she carried it when she hunted.

At the moment I figured out real quick, I was the game, and if I didn't do a little scamperin', tellin' her what happened, I was going to end up with an ass-full of buckshot. Or worse yet, dead on my own front steps.

I held up my hands like I'd seen them criminals do on *Cops*. "Give me a chance to tell ya the story at least."

"Tell," she said, gesturing with the barrel of my gun.

"Can't we go inside so I can sit?" I didn't want to say nothin' about how the whiskey was makin' me feel right about then.

"Tell."

That time the gun gesture she made got her point out *real* clear like. She didn't care about no fog or cold or dark night. She just wanted to know where the hell I'd been and what the hell I'd been doin'.

I took a deep breath of the thick air and figured the best place to start my tellin' was at Benny's, a bar down on Owl Creek Road, right near the Miller place. Benny owned Benny's, ran it like every drop of booze was the most important drop of booze on the planet, never givin' no man a free drink for no reason. Cheap

bastard, but a hard-worker and I liked him for that.

Benny had one of my elk heads, a seven-pointer, on the wall over the pool table. I was damn proud of that head, and spent many an evenin' in there drinkin' and starin' at it and makin' sure no one hit it with a pool cue.

"I was at Benny's," I told her.

Ethel snorted, clearly not surprised.

"Two Buds and then I left, I swear. I was aheadin' home for dinner by half-past six."

"Dinner got ate at seven," she said, the anger in her voice so strong that behind me I imagined I could feel the trees startin' to shake with fear. I know I was, but I couldn't be showin' her any weakness and I couldn't be upchuckin' no cookies from being sick on the whiskey. I had to keep on talkin' and talkin' fast.

"Tossed your dinner out at nine," Ethel said. "I let the dog eat it."

I wanted to ask her if the dog liked it, or if the dog was even still alive, but

figured real quick-like to just not be saying anythin' real stupid with her still holdin' my shotgun. So I just nodded like I understood and kept on tellin'.

"I was walkin' down Owl Creek, headin' home after only two Buds, when this bright light comes at me from over the trees like a big bird diving for a rabbit. That there light just sort of hovered right smack over the road above me. I tell ya Ethel, that there light was so bright I had to go and cover my eyes."

She grunted.

I was sure she wasn't believin' me, but the story had to be as I started it, since changin' the tellin' now would cause me even more problems, and more problems at three in the morning, facin' an angry woman with a shotgun, is not somethin' any man wants.

So I just went right on, makin' the details real thick-like, cause I heard once that details make a story sound more right.

"And there was this wind," I told her, swingin' my arms up and around as if I was a warmin' up to throw something, "like that storm we had last winter that knocked down the chicken coop. I tell you, that there wind was real strong like, blowing dust into my face."

"No wind here," she said.

"The wind was a comin' right out of the light."

"Oh," she said.

"Then suddenly the light just sort of grabbed me and picked me up and sucked me through this big hole and into this really big room that was real dark considering it was inside the bright light."

She grunted and I didn't much blame her, since this was soundin' a might stupid to me. What on God's green earth had made me think tellin' her the truth about gettin' taken by aliens would stop her from shootin' me? But I was committed to the tellin' and I figured right then and there that the only way to get this out was to just tell her fast, before she decided I was too stupid to live and just shot me. Dyin' from a blast with my own shotgun just wasn't my idea of how to leave this life.

Takin' another deep breath to push back the whiskey-dizzies, I went on.

"I was frozen like a deer in a truck's headlights, standin' there starin' at three little gray guys, little fella's no taller than my belt, skinny, big long fingers, just like they had on the tee-vee in that movie we saw last year. You know the one with all them aliens?"

She stared at me and just said nothin' and when Ethel says nothin' I knew buckshot and a quick burial was a comin' next. You didn't go messin' with Ethel, and I doubted if Sheriff Bob would even bother to arrest her for killin' me once he heard why she had done it.

It was three in the mornin' and I was whiskey stupid and didn't have a lick of sense to begin with anyway, so I kept on tellin' her about the aliens.

"One of these little guys with only three long fingers took my hand and walked me across the room to a table and then pointed to a chair. I remember readin' in the *Enquirer* that they usually did things no man wants done, but they didn't seem to have read the same issue I read, which pleased me a might I can tell you. I sat right down let me tell you, since I was scared plain out of my wits and about ready to dump a big one in my pants."

Ethel just grunted and shook her head.

"The three little guys went around the table, each a sittin' on one of the other sides. They must have had booster chairs under them because they could see over the edge of the table and look me right in the face with their big, slanted eyes. The one closest to me pointed at the plate in front of him and then at me."

Ethel hadn't moved, even to shift her bulk from one swollen foot to the other, which for Ethel was some special thing. I knew that if I managed to get out of this alive I'd be rubbin' her feet for a week.

She made that gesture that said I should go on, so I did. "Right then I noticed that the table was set like for a special Sunday dinner, with white plates, silverware, and food, lots of food, and it smelled real nice as well, like that wonderful turkey you made us last Thanksgivin'."

Figured a compliment or two couldn't hurt any, but it didn't even get her to blink, so I kept on with my tellin' real fast-like.

"It seemed they wanted me to try some of that there food in front of me, since the little fella next to me kept pointin' at the plate and then at me. The plates in front of them didn't have no food on them, but it seemed they wanted me to eat anyway. Now let me tell you, Ethel, I wasn't real pleased with the idea of eatin' no dinner fixed by little gray guys with three fingers who traveled in some beam of light. And I didn't hanker much to eatin' alone while they watched, but I figured I had no choice right about that point."

"You tellin' me you had dinner on an alien space ship?" Ethel asked, my gun moving in her arms more than I wanted it to move.

I ignored her question because that was just what I was about to tell her that I'd gone and done.

"When I picked up the fork on the outside like I had seen on that movie, they all clicked like a bunch of crickets, only louder, so I put the fork back down and they stopped clickin' and just stared instead."

Ethel just shook her head.

"It's gettin' cold out here," I said, easing my way up completely on the second step. "How's about I finish this at the table?"

"Keep on goin'," she said. "I don't want no blood in my house if I have ta go on and shoot ya."

I wanted to say it wasn't her damned double-wide, it was mine, since I had bought and paid two-thousand good, hard-earned money for it long before we had gone and gotten married, but contradictin' a woman with a shotgun had never been good thinkin'.

"Well, Ethel, let me tell you this," I said, going back to what had happened up there in that there spaceship, "I picked that fork back up and they went to clickin' again, stopped when I put it down, started when I picked it up, like there was somethin' really important about that there fork."

I took a deep breath and kept right on, not even lookin' at Ethel.

"Finally I got tired of playin' with 'em, so I just dug the fork into what looked like mashed potatoes with brown gravy and shoved a bite into my mouth like I hadn't eaten in days. Clickin'? You ain't never heard so much alien clickin', but I didn't much care because them there mashed potatoes were the best damned potatoes I had ever tasted, even better than the ones your Aunt Sarah used to make with that real butter that she took down to the church socials."

"You tellin' me you ate some alien's *food?*" Ethel asked.

"Every bite on the plate. Turkey drumstick, dressin', potatoes and gravy, roll, wanted to lick the plate it was all so good."

"You're eatin' while the perfectly good food I had worked hard to fix up for you sat gettin' cold on the table?"

"I couldn't help it," I said. "It weren't my idea to get sucked up into that light and set down at that table and clicked at. I just did as them there little fellas wanted me to do."

"And them there lipstick marks on your overalls?" she asked, swingin' my shotgun around to point at my chest that was covered in red marks that looked like a woman's lipstick. "Them from the little fellas as well?"

"They are at that," I said. "After I finished eaten that there food they had given me, all three of them got up and came over and started puttin' their three fingers on me all over and clickin' like mad. It was their fingers that left these here marks."

I pulled my coveralls away from my body and sort of held the chest part out for her to look at. "See, these here ain't no woman's lips. You can see for yourself they're alien fingerprints. Just look nice and close."

Again Ethel snorted and didn't move.

It was them there alien fingerprints that I was a hopin' would prove to her that my story was true and all. Alien fingerprints are damned hard to ignore I figure.

"So why did they want some fella like you?" Ethel asked.

"Directions," I said. "Them little guys were flat lost."

"The only place you know directions to is Benny's."

"Not true," I said. "Remember when we was lost two years ago, up in the hills and I got us out."

"Luck," she said, disgusted and waving the shotgun for me to go on tellin'.

"Well, it seemed that all their touching was a way of talkin'." I held out a section of my overalls to make sure she could still see the little red marks. "Ya

The First Two Cold Poker Gang Novels
Available at your favorite booksellers.

Now Available
from all your favorite booksellers
in trade paper and electronic editions.

see, them there little guys was warriors, soldiers, fighting in this big ol' war goin' on between them and these real ugly stick-like slug-creatures. I could see it all because it was like they was a runnin' a movie in my head."

I shuddered rememberin' it all, but kept on. "I could see the fightin' and killin' so clear, and let me tell you, them stick-slugs were ugly and really tall. Hell, I wanted to jump in right there and offer to help them there little gray fellas fight them ugly slugs. So I did."

"You did *what?*"

I took a deep breath and just kept on tellin' her the truth. "I up and said I'd help 'em in their war."

Ethel just shook her head and the shotgun swung around at me again. I wasn't going to get a chance to die for them gray guys. Ethel was going to kill me first. And I bet they didn't give out no ribbons for gettin' killed tellin' your wife the truth.

"Let me just finish, will ya?"

She shrugged, so I went on.

"Like I said, them little fellas was really lost, so that's all they wanted, but let me tell you, they was touched I offered to fight with them."

"You're the one who's touched," Ethel said.

"You just go and wait until them there big tall slug fellas start marchin' up the driveway. They fire light beams that can cook ya faster than Uncle Ben's barbecue pit."

She snorted. Not a good sign when Ethel starts snortin'.

"Look, I am knowin' you don't believe any of this, but what I saw when them there little gray guys touched me really opened my eyes, let me tell ya. This here is the battlefield. This country, this planet. All around us, right here, only

not really here where we can see it, but yet right here. You know, like when a dog can hear a whistle and we can't?"

Ethel didn't say anythin', which was a degree worse than snortin'.

I pointed at a tree. "One of them there tall skinny slugs could just come right out of that trunk right there and we'd both be dead. Them little gray guys called it somethin' like multi-dimension or somethin' *Twilight Zone-ish.*"

Ethel glanced at the tree.

"But the little gray guys seem ta know when the tall stick-slugs are a comin' and where and they keep 'em from doin' that, which is why I up and offered ta help."

"How can an idiot like you help them?" Ethel asked, disgusted.

"Guide," I said. "They showed me a map of the area and somehow, with all the clickin' and touchin', got me to understand they was a lookin' for a dock at Steven's Lake. I pointed right on one of their maps where it was at and we got there in a flash of white light, and let me tell you, just in time to stop them there stick-slugs from comin' out. Stick-slugs blow up like popcorn under the little gray guys' weapons, which would be just horrible for huntin' but great for killing enemy stick-slugs. After they was all done fightin', I was a hero and they offered me more food, but I told 'em I had to be gettin' on home."

"So, how come you're not still fighten' with them if you're such a hero?"

"I said I'd try to get more help and then be here when they needed me."

"Help?" Ethel asked. "You're gonna' tell other folks this story?"

"Sure," I said. "Told them there little gray guys I would, get more guides, get a few folks like me workin' for 'em. So they let me go, right back through the white light and onto the road where they'd taken me. I sort of staggered back to Benny's and since it was right before two in the mornin', I caught Benny before he closed up and had a couple of whiskies to calm my nerves. And then I came straight on home, I swear."

I put up my right hand like I was on one of them tee-vee court shows where people argue and yell and have all sorts of fun.

Ethel just shook her head and stepped toward me, grabbing my overalls and lookin' at the red marks. Then finally she said, "You're sleepin' with the dog."

"Now hold on there," I said, but she swung the shotgun around to point directly at me.

"It's three in da morning," she said, "and you been drinkin' and playin' pool and missed my dinner because you're a damn fool drunk. And if that there raspberry rubbin' don't come out of your overalls, I'm goin' ta make ya wear them anyway."

She turned and before I could get another word out of my mouth, she went inside and slammed the door on me. Can't say as I blamed her for not believin' my story.

I turned and whiskey-stumbled down off the two steps and headed for the dog house which I had built when we got the mutt a few years back. It weren't really no dog house, just a lean-to against the chicken coop, but the dog liked it and who was I to argue with a dog. I was a goin' to be covered in fleas by mornin', but I suppose that's not as bad as an ass full of buckshot.

I had made it halfway to the doghouse when a bright light hit me from overhead, a wind whipped up dust and dirt, and then the next damn thing I knew I was back in the alien ship with the three little fellas

clickin' at me. I was swayin' dizzy-like from the whiskey and the ride on the light.

I can't say I was happy to be seein' them again so fast, but after facin' Ethel and that shotgun, they looked pretty darned harmless.

This time they wanted me to try some really nice-tastin' ice cream. Strawberry, with swirls right in there of some sort a chocolate. Ethel would end up even bigger if she ever laid her hands on the fixin' for that there stuff. They studied every move my spoon made like I was an artist at the ice-cream-eatin' event in the alien Olympics.

And I can tell ya, my spoon did some real fancy dancin'. After three full dishes of the stuff, I waved off a fourth, then with them gettin' more red marks on my coveralls, I told them where Deacon Creek Falls were. They let me lay down and catch a few winks while they went and killed more stick-slugs, since ice cream and whiskey don't match if you do much movin' around after, and I couldn't see how I'd be much use in a fight throwin' up and all.

They finally woke me up with a bunch of loud clickin' and shot me through the light back by the dog house.

It was a comin' up on dawn and Ethel was already up and cookin' breakfast, so I just went on inside. She pointed at the table just like them aliens had, only without clickin', and served me my favorite breakfast, buttermilk pancakes smothered in maple. She never mixed up a batch of buttermilks unless something was wrong, or she really needed somethin' from me. And after the tellin' of my story, I had no idea what that might be.

I ate as much of them as I could, and let me tell ya that wasn't no easy chore after a night of doin' nothin' but eatin'.

I kept waitin' for her to say whatever she wanted, because with Ethel I could always tell when something was runnin' around on her mind, but she just watched me eat in silence, no talkin', no clickin' and didn't say nothin' about my story, and I didn't go tellin' her about my ice cream visit to the little fellas and hours of sleep on the alien ship. I figured she wouldn't have believed me no-how.

Besides, there was just no point in gettin' in even more trouble for not sleepin' in the doghouse.

Finally, after I just couldn't eat another bite she spoke her mind. "You go back, get me them recipes."

I stared at her like she had gone and lost her grip on reality.

"Recipes?" I asked. "There's a war on, woman."

"I don't care about no war," she said. "You can help them or not, make me no mind. But I want them alien mashed potatoes recipe, and the dressing one if you can get it, too. Monthly social is a comin' up and…"

She stopped like she knew I knew what she was a sayin'. I couldn't believe my luck. She had just up and gave me a free ticket to husband heaven. She needed me to get her somethin', and from the looks of the buttermilk pancakes, she was a willin' to pay. I was goin' ta be eatin' good for a week. And havin' my beer toted to me in my chair in front of the tee-vee. And no more doghouse for stoppin' at Benny's every night. Any darned time I wanted somethin' all I had to say was I was a tryin' to get her them there alien recipes.

"Next time them little fellas come and get me for some eatin', and guidin'" I said, nodding to her real serious and all, "I'll ask them. How does that sound ta ya?"

She gave me her sad smile and shook her head, which puzzled me for a moment. Then she stood, moved over to the stove

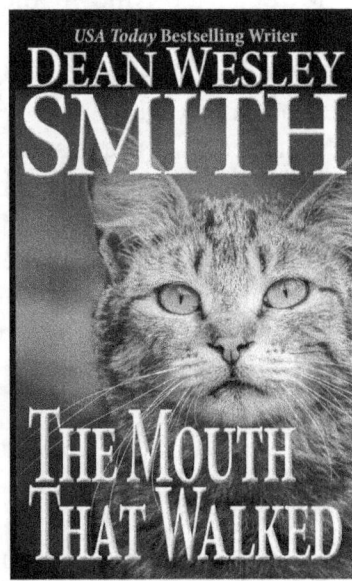

Some Classic Dean Wesley Smith Stories
Available at your favorite booksellers.

and pulled out my shotgun from a spot she'd hidden it.

"You were supposed to be a sleepin' in the doghouse," she said, pointing the gun right into my face, "so where was ya? And don't go tellin' me ya went back to them aliens for dessert. There ain't no aliens, no recipes, just you, an old drunk lyin' to his wife. So no lyin'. Where was ya? Widow Matti?"

I should have known Ethel wouldn't have gone and believed me, since she never read *The National Inquirer.* She didn't know them there gray guys got folks from all over the country ta help them in their big fight with the tall stick-slugs.

The visions of my husband heaven left me like a cat being chased by a dog. Now she thought I was a cheatin' on her with the widow Matti.

But I had to tell her the truth. I just couldn't think of anythin' else while lookin' down the barrel of my shotgun.

"I'm not a cheatin' on ya. Them there little fellas took me in the light again, gave me ice cream, asked directions to Deacon Creek Falls, and let me sleep on the floor. I swear!"

The red in her face sort of crawled up from her thick neck like a burner on the stove gettin' hot.

I held up my hands as the business end of that shotgun sort of got bigger. "Okay, wait, wait, I stumbled into the woods to toss my cookies and passed out near the woodpile."

"Checked there," she said, her face gettin' redder and startin' ta look like a ripe tomato.

I was about as desperate as a man could get, and my brain was a workin' on too little sleep and too much food and didn't seem ta be helpin' like it was

supposed ta be in a husband crisis. So, without really doing much thinkin' I shouted out what she wanted ta hear.

"Okay, okay I was at widow Matti's cabin, and she rode me like a cowboy rides a bull, and I can even show you her spur marks in my side if ya want."

Ethel's face was about as red as I had ever seen it.

I glanced around at the door, figurin' that if I made the outside and ducked right, she might miss me enough with the shot for me to live. But if Ethel was anythin', she was a fine shot, and I just wasn't that fast.

I was just about to make my break when suddenly the build-up exploded, but not like I had 'spected. She burst out laughin' and lowered the shotgun.

I stared at her, more stunned than I had remembered feelin' starin' at them there three little gray men inside the light. She was laughin' and shakin' her head and the flesh on her arms was a movin' in all sorts of directions like waves on a beach. It was like Jay Leno had just told a joke right there in the kitchen.

"What's so danged funny?" I asked after she managed to catch a breath.

"Your story," she said, startin' to laugh all over again. After a moment she just shook her head. "You and the widow Matti. Now *that's* funny."

"Why is *that* so danged funny?" I asked.

The widow Matti had given me a few looks, but I sure hadn't told Ethel that, and I wasn't a bad-lookin' man, even if I didn't shave much and wore the same shirt for a few days in a row.

"Stick with them aliens servin' ya food story," Ethel said, shaking her head and startin' to clean up the kitchen. "And when I tell ya ta sleep in the doghouse, you better get your ass in there real pronto-like."

I opened my mouth to say somethin' real smart back in return, then decided that anythin' I might say wasn't real smart at that point, which is a good rule to follow just about any time with Ethel, but especially now after I had lied to her about bein' ridden by another woman, so instead I just sat right there at the kitchen table and nodded like a toy dog in the back window of a pick-up truck.

Still, it hurt that she didn't believe her own husband would be somethin' the widow Matti might ride some night. The widow had taken on old Chester from the service station, or at least Chester claimed she had every time he had a few too many drinks.

I believed Chester, yet my own damned wife didn't believe me about the widow Matti or about them there aliens either. Or the war with the tall stick-slugs. Maybe next time them little guys took me up into the light for dinner and directions, I *would* ask them for the recipe for them there mashed potatoes.

Then I'd give that there recipe to the widow Matti.

I bet the widow Matti would be real grateful like, and maybe give me a ride like she'd done to Chester. Especially when she found out I was a real war hero and all, keepin' the world safe from them stick-slug invasions.

The widow Matti would go and believe me. And then that would show Ethel.

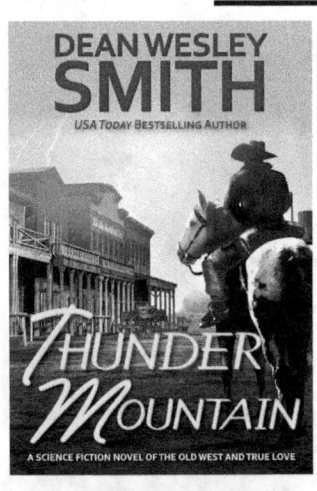

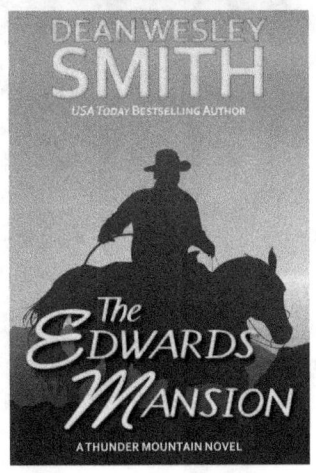

USA TODAY BESTSELLING AUTHOR

DEAN WESLEY SMITH

LAYING THE MUSIC TO REST

A former college professor turned bartender, Doc finds himself trying to save his friends from a ghost under a lake in the wilderness of Idaho.

From diving into a ghost town buried under a lake to trying to stay alive on the sinking deck of the Titanic, this time-travel science fiction novel reads like a roller-coaster ride with all the twists and turns.

First published in paperback in 1989 from Warner Questar Books, Dean Wesley Smith's first published novel gives a lot of hints of his future series and his bestselling career spanning over a hundred and fifty novels.

Published here in its original form, without any changes, just as Dean wrote it almost thirty years ago.

LAYING THE MUSIC TO REST

Part 1

PROLOGUE

Roosevelt, Idaho
May, 1909

THE BITING, COLD water of flooded Monumental Creek twisted Gretchen's dress around her legs as she fought to open the front door of the Roosevelt Inn.

"Alex!" she shouted at the wood. "Alex! Open the door."

The black night, the steady drumming of the rain, and the sadistic rustle of the swirling water swallowed her shout as if it hadn't existed. She banged her fist against the wood, but even that was muffled as the dark, empty town seemed to laugh at her.

She took a deep breath, yanked her dress up so that the hem rode around her knees, and braced her left foot against the edge of a board in the sidewalk. She pushed slowly. The door wouldn't move. Frustrated, she rammed her shoulder into the door. Her foot slid on the wood and she went to her knees in the icy water.

"Alex," she called again as the current pulled at her. Her cold fingers found the doorframe and she held on. Alex was waiting for her. She had to get to him. She levered herself back to her feet, then carefully tested the door one last time. Solid.

She took a deep, shuddering breath and tried to make herself relax against the cold. She'd only been wading in the water a few minutes. The sharp, jabbing pain she had felt when she first stepped into the water had faded to a constant dull ache.

She took another breath and forced herself to think. Frank. That was the problem. He must have bolted the front door after they took the last of the supplies up to the tent. He probably figured it would help keep the water away from the piano. The back door was two steps higher and she had been one of the last out that way. She was sure it was open.

She quickly splashed her way along the covered front of the Inn, down the two steps, and into the rain and deeper water. Thick mud from the street oozed up and over her shoes and sucked at her feet, trying to pull her into the muck. Moving carefully so that the mud wouldn't yank her shoes off, she turned into the narrow alley that ran between the south side of the Inn and the next building.

In the summer months, miners too drunk to make it back to their diggings slept along this wall, sometimes four or five at a time. Now the icy water swirling around her thighs tried to push her from between the buildings, billowing her skirt and slips in front of her like sails in a strong wind.

Ahead she could faintly see the dark edges of the two buildings and beyond that the black mass of the steep mountainside. The roar of the swollen creek echoed down the narrow alley, warning her to turn back. But she couldn't. She had to find Alex. Using both hands, one on each building to steady herself, she pushed slowly forward.

As she neared the back of the Inn, a chunk of wood banged hard against her knees and tangled in her skirt. She reached down to free it, lost her balance, and fell. The cold water closed over her and crushed the breath from her lungs. Her mouth filled with muddy water. The current shoved her back toward Main Street. She jammed one foot down into the mud and pushed herself out of the water.

She pressed both numbed hands against the rough logs of the two buildings and forced herself to wait for her breath to return. She wasn't going to let the water stop her. Not now.

Bracing herself with one hand, she leaned against the Inn, brushed her hair from her face, and then felt for the hand mirror strapped under her soaking dress. Alex's mirror. She had tied it inside her corset against her stomach. It was lucky she had. If she dropped it now, she'd never find it in the black water.

She did a careful check to make sure the mirror was still solidly pressed against her, almost warm inside her soaking dress. Only six hours ago she had seen the mirror for the first time. Six long hours since Alex first pulled out the carved, ivory-framed glass and held it up proudly for her to see. The day might have turned out to be the best day of her life if she hadn't been such a fool.

***

The cold, rainy morning had started with the entire town wild with the rumor that one of the packing outfits had finally made it over the Dewey Summit with supplies from Idaho City. After seven months of being snowbound in the narrow Monumental Valley, that was celebration news.

Gretchen had decided to wear her finest dress for that special night. Alex also dressed for dinner in his finest, coming down to town wearing a Boston lawyer's suit. She thought he looked more handsome than ever, if that was possible.

All the girls said Alex was the best catch in the valley. With his suits, fancy English, and smoky blue eyes, he could have any free woman he chose. But in seven months he had paid attention only to Gretchen. He had been perfectly polite and honorable. And even though she was a saloon piano player, he treated her as if she were a Boston lady.

That night he had come into the Inn at his normal dinner hour and asked if he might have a moment with her after everything had quieted down.

At first the request had excited her. But then, as the evening wore on and she watched him eat his dinner and sip his brandy, she began to worry. What did he want? Was he leaving town now that the pass was open? Why did he seem so serious? Unanswered questions from the winter came flooding back. What was he doing in Roosevelt? What did he see in her? What did he want from her? She was just a saloon girl and he was a Boston gentleman. They could never be together. She was sure he must know that.

But he thought otherwise. He used his grandmother's beautiful mirror to ask her to marry him.

She had said no.

***

She banged her fist against the wall of the Inn and moved carefully toward the back door. Why hadn't she said yes? She had been so afraid and so stupid.

But Alex would not give up. He would come back for her. She knew it. He would be inside the Inn, waiting. This time she would tell him yes.

She reached the back door of the Inn. It stood wide open and the water level was at her knees. The men had better get that mudslide cleared. The water was filling the narrow valley faster than she had imagined possible.

She moved inside the black room and along the wall toward the sink. Jim had left one lantern hanging there in case someone had to come back. She reached the sink and leaned against it for a moment, trying to catch her breath. The cold water had forced a throbbing ache up into her stomach, radiating out under her arms and across her chest in a dull web of pain. She could hardly breathe. She needed to get out of the water and into dry clothes soon. Alex had to be there.

"Alex!" she shouted into the dark, water-filled room. Her voice sounded funny, as if she were in a deep mine shaft. He didn't answer.

He hadn't been in his cabin or down with the men working to clear the mudslide. He had to be at the Inn, waiting for her. That was where he had disappeared, vanished like a wisp of smoke right before her eyes. One minute he had asked her to marry him and the next he had simply faded away, as if he had only been a dream and she was waking up.

But she had not been asleep. He would come back, that she was sure of. She could feel it. He would come back to the Inn, to the very place where he had disappeared. She knew that, too. She didn't know why. She just knew. She touched the hard surface of the mirror. She would have his grandmother's mirror for him when he did. She would wait.

She found the lantern and pulled it from the hook. It seemed unusually heavy in her numb fingers. She held it and felt carefully on the ledge over the sink for the block of matches. They were still dry, so she broke off one match and scraped it against the rough wood of the wall.

The match caught on the second try and the sudden blues and yellows outlined against the darkness blinded her. She lit the lantern, her fingers like logs against the thin chimney glass. After the wick caught, she held her hands over the warmth and looked around the room she had worked and lived in for the past seven months.

In six hours it had become so different. Black water filled the room, with small twigs and leaves floating in quick currents. The four beds that usually stood against the south wall had floated over into the back corner. A blanket lay half on, half off one bed and a black stain showed where the water had soaked up into the cotton.

She lifted the lantern off the counter and waded toward the door leading into the main room. The pain in her legs made her feel as if she were walking on stumps. Only the jarring in her groin told her when her feet touched the floor.

The door to the main room was closed and latched. She fumbled with the bolt before she got it open and stepped up onto the platform that held her piano.

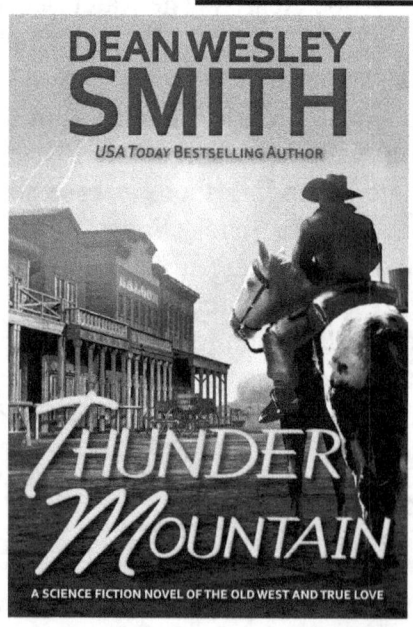

The pale light from the single lantern cast dark shadows across the flooded main room of the Inn. Tables still occupied their correct positions, but every so often the water shifted one of the chairs as if some unseen patron still sat on it.

The potbellied stove against the stairs looked cold and black, its door open, its fire out. The long liquor shelves behind the bar were ugly, empty scars on the face of the north wall. The room was no longer the warm, lively place she had filled with music all winter long.

The table closest to the piano was where Alex had sat. Where he had asked her to marry him. Where he had disappeared. When he had started to fade away, she'd screamed and tried to hold him. But he had been like a ghost. She could see the front wall through his chest and her hands passed through him like a cold draft through an open window.

Frank had been upstairs to allow her and Alex some privacy. The rest of the girls had already gone to bed in the back. Her screams as Alex vanished had brought everyone running. No one believed that he had disappeared. No one.

They had put her in bed by the time the alarm came about the mudslide. Frank had gone to take a look, and when he got back he looked white and scared. There was a huge mudslide coming down Mule Creek from the direction of the Dewey Mine. It was traveling almost as fast as a man could walk.

He had everyone take all they could carry and follow him. They put up a tent about a half mile upstream on higher ground, then made three trips to get the liquor, plates, silverware, clothes, and valuables. By the time they made the last trip, the flowing wall of mud and rock had dammed the main valley a hundred yards below the town and the water from the heavy rains and the spring melt was already a foot deep on Main Street.

Gretchen had wanted Frank to move the piano to higher ground, too. But Frank had decided that it was a better gamble to put all their efforts into trying to clear a channel around the slide. The next few hours had echoed with the sound of dynamite explosions as the men fought the moving mud and rock. Now, except for the rain and the constant roar of Monumental Creek, the valley was still.

Gretchen had been unable to stay in the tent. She knew Alex was out there somewhere. All she had to do was find him and tell him she had changed her mind. She would ask him to forgive her. She would tell him that she would be honored to be his wife and go to Boston with him.

But he hadn't been at his cabin or working at the slide. He had disappeared from the Inn. That was where he would return. She knew it.

She set the lantern down on the piano and held her hands over the flame to get whatever warmth she could. Then she opened three buttons of her dress, carefully untied the corset strings she had used to hold the mirror tight against her stomach, and pulled the mirror into the lamp light.

The ornately carved patterns in the ivory handle and frame seemed to dance in the flickering light as she held the mirror up. It was like nothing Gretchen had ever seen. Alex had mentioned that the mirror had been in his family for generations. His grandfather had used it to propose to Alex's grandmother, and Alex's father had used it to propose to Alex's mother. Tonight, Alex had used it to ask her to join his image in the mirror and be his wife. She had turned the mirror face down on the table. Refused his offer.

"I'm sorry, Alex," she said softly. The room didn't even allow an echo of an answer.

"Please, Alex. Come back."

A fit of shivering caught her. A chair near the front door swung a half turn around, startling her. The building groaned, as if it too wanted to move. She shivered again. If Alex came, he could help her back to the tent and she could get into some dry clothes. Maybe if she played for him, he would hear her.

Using both hands, she slid the mirror face up onto the top of the piano. Then she pulled the bench out. It floated free and started to tip over. She held it against the floor while she moved between it and the piano and sat down.

Carefully she moved the mirror down onto the music rack in front of her, then slid the bench to get into her normal position. Water splashed up on the keyboard. She tried to wipe the drops of water off with the lace on her sleeve. When Alex got back, she would talk to him about getting some men and saving the piano. She couldn't let it get ruined. Not after all the work of getting it over the pass. She had kept such good care of it all winter.

She tried a sample chord with her shaking hands. The sound felt much fuller, louder, as if the watery room wanted to keep the music alive and holding its tone long after she released the keys.

She hit another chord and then tried to run a simple scale. Her fingers were so numb, they got in each other's way. She felt as if they weren't even a part of her body. She couldn't feel her feet and legs.

She pulled the lamp on the piano directly in front of her and held her hands over the chimney. After a moment she could feel the heat biting into her skin.

She rubbed her fingers together, then held them over the lamp again. She repeated the process until she could feel tingling in her fingertips. She wished she could do the same for her legs. They were nothing more than logs hanging off her body in the water. She'd have to play without using the pedals.

She sat up straight on the bench, arched her back, and tried to clear the thick fog from her mind. She placed both hands lightly on the keyboard and looked down at the table where Alex had last sat. She tried to imagine him reappearing there, fading back into the room just as slowly as he had faded out. She would play his favorite song for him. Then he would return.

The first note filled the room and the song flowed perfectly. Not once during the entire piece did she look away from the table. And when the last note died in the black of the water, she felt empty. Lost.

She slumped against the piano and looked around. She could feel that Alex was there. She didn't know how, but she knew he was close.

She held the mirror up. He was there, with her, and yet he wasn't. She stared into the mirror until she felt dizzy and had to lean her head against the hard wood of the piano to get the spinning to stop.

The water lapped over the top of the bench. She felt as if her entire body were draining out of her legs. Alex was close. If she played his favorite song once more, he would return and take her to someplace warm and hold her and tell her he wanted her for his wife. She needed to play his song again so he could hear her.

She took a few quick breaths to try to calm the shuddering that racked her shoulders before warming her shaking fingers over the lamp. Then she started the song once more, only this time she looked into the mirror, seeing Alex's face in it.

She played the song. His song. And when she was finished, she started over, playing it again. And then again, until finally her hands would work no more.

She tried to warm her fingers over the lamp, but her head was spinning so much that she misjudged and knocked the lamp sideways, out of reach. She tried to stand and grab for it before it fell, but her legs were nothing more than weights attached to her body. Her sudden lunge shifted the bench and tipped her sideways.

The lamp rolled off the piano, hit the water, and with a hiss plunged the room into total blackness. Thrashing wildly to regain her footing, Gretchen too slipped under.

Her mind screamed for her to find a handhold, get her breath. The cold crushed what little air she had left out of her chest and she tasted the muddy water.

Finally she caught the edge of the keyboard and pulled herself up into the air. But her legs refused to move under her and her fingers were too weak to hold on.

She slipped a second time. The room held the sound of her struggle like it had held the music moments before, kicking it from wall to wall, savoring it, holding it out for the empty tables and the cold stove to inspect.

She grasped the side of the piano and slowly pulled her head back above the black surface.

"Alex?" she whispered.

But the room refused her, killing even the faintest echo of her plea. Her fingers could not hold on to the polished wood long. After a moment she dropped into the black cold.

Silence again took over the room.

CHAPTER ONE

Boise, Idaho
June 25, 1990

"ALL RIGHT, DOC," Angie said as she pushed open the back door of the Garden Restaurant and Lounge and dropped two grocery sacks on the kitchen counter. "What happened today?"

Not even a simple good morning. I shook my head, trying to contain a smile. "Not a thing yet. But I could cut myself and get it over with." I held up the knife I had been using to slice limes.

"Thanks for the offer," she said. "But I think Tuesday will give us more than enough thrills." She glanced around. "Smells good in here. You must have made it up for the bread."

"Beat the truck by five minutes. I should have slept longer."

She laughed. "I'll be hiding in the office doing the damn withholding taxes. Let me know when the coast is clear."

"Give it time. It's only eleven."

She grabbed the smallest of the two sacks and tapped the remaining one. "Bar rags. Nice and clean. Just like the old man ordered." She stuck her tongue out at me and then turned and headed for the office.

I laughed as she ducked past the sinks and down the back hall, acting as if I might throw something at her at any moment. She loved teasing me about my recent fortieth birthday. Probably because she knew it bothered me.

I loved Angie as if she were my sister. She was single, thirty-two years old, and the shortest woman I had ever met.

Well-proportioned, people said. I remember thinking the same thing the very first time I saw her walk into my class.

She'd been a student of mine ten years ago and somehow, over the years, we had managed to become friends. She and my wife, Carla, had hit it off from the moment they met. Six months after Carla died, Angie and I decided to buy the Garden. It was one of those "what-the-hell" decisions. Angie had money to invest from her divorce settlement and I was sick of teaching at the university. We both needed the change and the Garden had looked like the ideal way to do it.

So for the last five years, I had done all the day bartending, becoming more and more bored and set in my ways. Even more than when I was teaching.

Angie's side of the partnership was to do the books and help out Friday and Saturday nights. In five years she hadn't missed a weekend and I'd never asked her if she was bored. And every damn Tuesday over those years something had gone wrong. Sometimes only little things. Sometimes major, like the Tuesday a year ago when we had the grease fire in the grill hood. Shut us down for over a week.

Besides all the happenings, I had another good reason for not liking Tuesdays. They delivered the bread on Tuesdays at nine in the morning, one hour before I usually had to be at work. One very long, very annoying hour. Someone had to meet the truck to give the driver a check. So Angie and I had agreed. She washed the bar rags. I met the bread truck. I swore every Tuesday morning as I climbed out of bed that I was getting the raw end of the deal.

This week it wasn't until after the lunch rush that Tuesday struck.

Angie had gone home for the afternoon "to hide," and the normal lunch crowd had left. I had just finished cleaning off the last table, had put a good jazz tape on the sound system, and was sitting at the bar reading the morning paper and eating my normal French-dip sandwich when the front door opened and Constance walked in.

Alone.

Just as simple as that, Tuesday struck. The little bit of the sandwich I had already eaten suddenly felt like a hundred pounds of rock pressing me into the bar stool. Something had happened to Fred.

I swiveled off the bar stool and went to meet her as she weaved her way in and out of the plants and tables. Constance was a robust woman, not really tall, but the way she held herself made her seem tall. She had a full head of curly gray hair, a deep, rich voice, and a smile that made others around her smile without reason. Today she wore tan slacks, a blue work shirt with the sleeves rolled up, and a blue ribbon that held her hair back away from her face.

Fred, her husband, was my best friend. We'd known each other since we were in the first grade. Believe me, I can't go back much further than that and still remember things.

Fred looked like a bald flagpole. At forty, he maintained his wiry look and incredible strength. Above my fireplace I had a picture of the three of us that Angie took a few years back. Constance, the shortest, was on the right. I was in the middle, wearing one of my usual thick sweaters. I had my beard and mustache trimmed a little closer then and my hair still had a lot more brown in it than gray. Fred, three inches taller than me, clean-cut and bald, was on my left. I always had the feeling that the picture was tipped slightly because of the way we were standing, short to tall.

During the winter, Fred and Constance both taught at a local high school and were regulars at the Garden. Every summer they would pack up and disappear into the rough central Idaho primitive area to work on small mining claim and some land they'd bought up there before the government locked it all up into wilderness. They were putting a lodge and six small cabins on it. This summer was to be their first season with what they liked to call "guests."

For the past three summers I had promised I would go in with them to take a look and maybe help out a little. Every summer something had come up. And not once in all those years had they come out of the primitive area until the week before school started. Yet suddenly, here was Constance without Fred. Something was big-time wrong.

I gave Constance the best rib-compressing hug I could, and she gave me a quick answer to my question—yes, Fred was all right and had just stayed back up at the lodge to watch the guests. I pointed to the stool beside mine and moved around behind the bar.

"You had lunch?" I asked as I poured Constance her regular drink—vodka Collins, only half the ice, lime garnish—then slid it in front of her.

She nodded. "In McCall. Two hours ago." She held up the drink. "Thanks." I nodded and then built myself an orange juice and soda and moved back around the bar.

I pushed my unfinished sandwich down the bar, out of the way. "I give up, I can't stand the suspense. If Fred's all right and you're all right, just what are you doing here?"

Constance laughed her deep, full laugh. "Always right to the point," she said. "One of the many things I love about you." She leaned over and kissed my check, the first time a woman had kissed me in a long time.

"Well, I'm here for three reasons. One, to talk to you. Two, to get supplies. And three, to place some new advertising. Always use more guests, you know."

Some Classic Jukebox Stories
Available at your favorite booksellers.

"You been getting some?" I tried to keep the disbelief out of my voice. I had always thought the idea of a lodge twenty miles inside the most rugged primitive area in the lower forty-eight was something on the other side of crazy. Of course, being crazy was part of Fred. But this idea was beyond even Fred's normal sense of looney. Hell, from the maps and pictures they had shown me, there wasn't a stretch in that valley wide enough or long enough to put a landing strip. The ranches down on the Salmon River at least had that. All of Fred and Constance's guests had to pack in on horseback. Or worse yet, walk.

Again Constance laughed. "Of course we are. At one point we had nine guests. Not bad for our first year."

I nodded, but I could tell now that Constance wasn't giving me the entire story. She had that little wrinkle above her eyes that she always used to get when she worried about Fred and me doing something stupid. Carla used to just frown and

shake her head. I hadn't seen that look on Constance in years. And it suddenly occurred to me that I had missed it.

"So why advertise? Isn't nine about maximum for what you've got built?"

She nodded. "But we only have two left." She took a long sip of her drink, then turned to face me. "That's why we need your help. Fred wanted to do it alone, but I wouldn't let him. I really don't like the idea of the both of you doing it, but—"

I touched Constance's arm. "Back up a minute. What was it Fred wanted to do alone? And exactly what is this about needing my help?"

"Sorry," she said, then laughed an uneasy laugh. "Fred wants to make a dive into the lake."

It felt as if the air conditioning had kicked on twenty degrees too low. The old mining claim they had bought ran along the side of a small mountain lake. The lake had been formed back in the early part of the century when a mudslide filled the narrow Monumental Valley and

backed water up over a booming mining town called Roosevelt. Constance had brought in pictures one September in which you could clearly see a huge log-jam that Fred claimed was the remains of the old buildings.

When they had first bought the claim I asked them why no one had ever heard of this huge disaster. It seemed to me that losing a town of over five thousand people would be a big deal. Yet the fact that it had happened had become one of those forgotten notes of Idaho history. Constance said the people down at the State Historical Society didn't even know much about it. It appeared that only Zane Grey, in his book *Thunder Mountain*, had even noticed and everyone thought that was just fiction.

"Into the old ghost town?" I asked. "Fred wants to dive into the old ghost town?" Fred had said a few years back that to his knowledge, no one had ever made a dive into the lake. The water was too cold, it was too tough to get equipment into the area, and it was just too dangerous. Twenty years ago Fred and I might have tried it. I didn't like the sound of it now.

Constance nodded. "There's not going to be much of any town down there. But he still wants to make the dive."

"Hell, that's crazy. Fred knows better than to think about making a dive alone, especially into a mountain lake like that. Anything could happen." The knot in my stomach that was clamped around the first few bites of my French-dip sandwich wasn't letting go. In fact, it was getting worse and I was getting slowly mad at Fred for even thinking about being so stupid. I'd lost Carla and losing Fred scared me more than I wanted to admit.

"Tell him that."

"I will," I said. "And damn loud. That fool knows better. Jesus, it's been ten years since either one of us strapped on a tank. What could be so important that he'd even think of making that dive alone?"

"Try twelve years," Constance said. "We figured it up one night. The last time you both did any diving was on that rescue operation over near the Snake. Remember?"

I nodded. I remembered real well. How could I forget? It hadn't been so much a rescue mission as pure and simple stupidity. A five-year-old boy went under in a millpond in front of two dozen witnesses. Two days and no one could find the body. Fred and I were called in by a friend of the family to help only because the regular Search and Rescue divers were needed elsewhere. From the report of what the body looked like when it finally did surface, we were damn lucky we couldn't find it. And once Fred ended up tangled in weeds for a good ten minutes before he could work his way free and surface.

For months I dreamed of that boy's bloated face appearing out of the muck of the pond in front of my facemask like some bad special effect in a slasher movie. On top of that, I didn't believe in risking lives in a weed-choked pond just to find a body that was going to float to the surface in a day or two anyway. The only thing that practice did was create more bodies.

Before that nightmare Fred and I had done a lot of diving. We had made excursions in the Gulf of Mexico, Canadian mountain lakes, and a bunch of places in between. Strapping on scuba tanks and exploring was one of the crazy things we prided ourselves in doing, even though it worried the hell out of both Carla and

Constance. I wondered what ever happened to our doing crazy things.

"So," I said after a long moment of silence interrupted only by the traffic sounds from Grove Street. "Why make a dive?"

"I'm not really sure, exactly," Constance said. She looked uncomfortable as she twisted her drink slowly in her strong hands. "Professor Jerome says that's what we need to do to help the ghost."

"I—hang on a minute." I swiveled away from Constance and went around behind the bar. She was making no sense at all. I built her a new drink, slid it across the bar, and then sat on the counter behind the bar so I could look directly at her. If whatever brought her into town was as complicated as it was beginning to seem, I wanted to be able to see her eyes. With Constance, everything came through her green eyes.

"All right," I said, "how about you starting from the beginning?"

Constance nodded, then finished her first drink, set it aside, and swirled the straws in the second. "You remember Fred mentioning that the lake was haunted?"

I nodded. A few years back they had returned with stories about a woman ghost walking around the lake. It had been the joke of the bar for most of that September. I remembered being surprised that they would even talk about such stuff, let alone act as if they believed it. That wasn't like Fred or Constance. I ended up not knowing what to believe and they never mentioned it again.

"Well, we weren't fooling," she said, "even though everyone thought we were. The ghost has been there right from the first time Fred and I camped at the old

mine site. With all the people who lived in Roosevelt before it was flooded, I guess a ghost or two should be expected. We got used to seeing her walking down along the old mudslide and then into the water. It just never occurred to us that she would be any more than a historical curiosity to our guests."

"She wasn't, I gather?" I didn't know what to make of this story. If it hadn't been Constance and she hadn't been sitting in the Garden in the middle of the summer, I would have laughed. I didn't feel close to laughing right now.

Constance shook her head slowly. "She doesn't hurt anything, except there's this mighty cold feeling if you get too close to her."

"I'll bet. Scared your customers?"

Constance nodded. "We had to refund a lot of money we were planning on using to build a seventh cabin up on the summit. Doesn't seem much reason to now, though. Not if she's going to keep spooking everyone."

"What about using her to bring in people? Seems to me if word got out about your ghost, there would be a lot of folks who would just love to see her."

"Crazies. The wrong kind of people. All we wanted was a place we could enjoy, back away from everything. The kind of people we want staying with us should want the same thing. Hiking. Fishing. Exploring. And lots and lots of quiet. That's not exactly what we would get if we had every weirdo in the country looking at our house ghost. Plus, imagine the fuss there'd be if she suddenly decided to not show up. It's not like we have any control over her."

For a moment Constance had a faraway look in her eyes and then she shook her head like a woman accepting the loss of a dream. "And now, with the guests going home and telling people, we might as well shut down next year."

I leaned back against the liquor cabinet. Constance was serious. I didn't believe what she was telling me, but at the same time I couldn't just laugh at her. "So she scared away all but two of your customers. What happened then?"

"No, she scared them *all* right back up over the summit. We have one new customer, a young woman who we warned about the ghost right up front. She doesn't seem to mind. And then Professor Jerome, who is our guest. He's from the University of California parapsychological studies department. We paid for him to fly into McCall. We picked him up there."

"You brought in a psychic? Fred agreed to this?" I just couldn't believe Fred would go for anything outside the reality of a tall bottle of Bud, a good game of chess, and a turkey sandwich.

"Not a psychic in the way you're thinking," Constance said. "Dr. Jerome is very respected and—"

"I know, I know," I said, waving away the obvious list of credentials Constance was about to spew all over

the bar. I had had my share of letters stenciled after my name on my old office door. The only good those letters had done was get me a little more money and intimidate the hell out of students. They might as well have been carved on my tombstone, for all the years I spent buried behind them. Deadly dull years. Fred should have known better than to be taken in.

"So what has this *professor* done so far?" I asked, not really wanting to hear the answer.

"Mostly just study the ghost," she said. "He's spent the last five days following her around the shore of the lake like a little puppy. He must have taken a hundred pictures and done who knows what with a couple strange-looking instruments with names too long for me to remember. He seems to think he knows what she wants."

Now I really wanted to laugh. It was everything I could do not to burst out right then. Constance was serious, I could tell that without a doubt. Her eyes didn't lie. But the thought of a ghost talking to some hokey professor from California was damn near too much. I forced my laughter back down like swallowing a bad pill and

ended up just shaking my head and then taking a long drink off my orange juice. Maybe I was getting too cynical. Fifteen years ago I might have bought this story. Why didn't I today?

Because it was too stupid to believe, that was why. The real question was why Fred was being sucked in by whatever scam this California nut was spouting. Not like Fred at all. No wonder Constance had come down to get me.

I sidestepped the part about the guy knowing what the ghost wanted and went back to my main question. "You still haven't told me why Fred wants to make a dive into the lake."

Constance sighed, stirred her drink for a moment, then looked up at me. "You're not going to believe it."

"I'm already having trouble," I said. "In case you haven't noticed. So you might as well hit me with everything."

"Professor Jerome says the ghost wants to find someone named Alex. There's something in the lake that might help. The professor thinks that if we find it, whatever it is might, as he calls it, let her rest."

"And Fred believes all this?" I had a clear look at Constance's eyes as she spoke. She believed everything she was saying. Everything. And I could tell she didn't like it any more than I did.

"Yes," she said, without hesitation.

"And you want me to make this dive with Fred to keep him from killing himself in that cold water?"

She nodded. "You know we wouldn't ask you to do something like this if it wasn't important."

"Fred would," I said.

Constance started to object until she saw I was kidding. I dropped down off the counter and fixed us both another drink, only this time I laced my orange juice and soda with vodka.

"You know how special the lodge is to us, don't you?"

"Of course," I said. "Hell, I should. Over the last few years it's been about the only thing you two could talk about."

Constance laughed. "It was going to be what got us out of that high school. You know, kind of like this place got you away from the university."

I wanted to tell her that this "escape" had ended up as bad as my original prison, but I didn't.

"With this ghost scaring away our good guests and maybe bringing in all the weird ones, the lodge won't end up being the quiet place we dreamed about. We've got to find a way to get rid of her. Somehow." Her voice trailed off like the end of a song.

"So Fred and I find whatever it is. What then? Does this professor fellow have any ideas?"

Constance shook her head. "None. Fred doesn't like the idea, either. I think that's why he wanted to do it alone. I think he's embarrassed. So am I, really. But we need to try something and we don't have any other obvious roads."

I nodded. There was really no decision for me to make. Three-quarters of my mind was scared silly at the idea of making a dive into a lake that had killed an entire town, especially with a "ghost" close by. A damn dumb thing to do by any standards.

But the rest of me was excited at the thought. Excited at the adventure, like I used to be when Fred and I did something the rest of the world considered crazy. And for some reason, right now that excitement scared me even more.

Scared or not, it was Fred and Constance and I couldn't say no. Besides, if the California professor was pulling a scam, I might be able to spot it.

"How long before the train pulls out?" I asked.

Constance laughed. "Five a.m. tomorrow morning."

"Ouch. Couldn't we at least make it seven?"

"Not unless you want to be riding a horse down a mountain in the dark."

"What the hell ever happened to getting up at a reasonable time?" I downed the last of my drink. "You got someone working on the diving gear?"

"Called the dive shop from McCall a few hours ago and gave them the list Fred put together. It will be ready at four this afternoon."

"Good. Then the next step is to call Angie and tell her Tuesday struck again. She's never going to believe this one."

"Tuesday?" Constance asked as I turned and headed for the phone in my office.

"Yeah," I said, trying to calm the twisting fear I felt starting to build in my stomach. "Around here we love Tuesdays."

To be continued...

USA *Today* Bestselling Writer

DEAN WESLEY SMITH

THEY WERE DIVIDED BY COLD DEBT

A Bryant Street Story

Bryant Street, a standard subdivision street, haunts us all. To escape Bryant Street often takes real courage.

Meet Neil Prendell. He made a mistake. He lost his job but avoided telling his wife. Instead, he pretended to go to work while looking for another job.

Pride? Fear? Stupidity? The reason no longer mattered. He paid the price.

A price that only made sense in the twisted logic of Bryant Street.

THEY WERE DIVIDED BY COLD DEBT
A Bryant Street Story

ONE

THE MAILBOXES IN his section of the Wilderness Park Subdivision all had stylized images of beavers on them cut out of metal. Every section of the subdivision had different animals on the mailboxes. And every mailbox was the same, just with slightly different numbers on their sides.

Every day that Neil Prendell drove off to his pretend job, he shook his head at the rows of identical metal beavers perched on top of the boxes as they mocked him.

And every day when he came home, they mocked him again.

It didn't help that he was coming home from a day of sitting in three different coffee shops searching for any possible job. He wasn't the only one in those shops searching, and he doubted he was the only lonely, desperate soul at those tables who hadn't told his wife that he had lost his job.

Times were bad for jobs.

Real bad.

Especially middle-management like him. His main skill was saying yes to one person and bossing others under him around. And he wasn't even that good at that, even with his MBA.

His goal had always been to be a guitar player in a band, but in the last year he hadn't even picked up his guitar.

He just didn't dare tell his wife Pam about losing his job. He had thought at first, he would find another one quickly and then tell her. In ten years of marriage, this home among the metal beavers had been the first time she had really been happy with him. Before he seemed to always not be good enough in her eyes.

And it had been her idea they both get MBAs. They had met in college when he was a music major. Her interest had always gone to real estate, but she had never really gotten the chance since college to work in the field. And now, with the recession hitting the housing so hard, he doubted she could find work either, even if she started looking.

So if he couldn't find another job and quickly, they would lose the house.

Lose their own very special beaver on the mailbox.

And more than likely, he would lose Pam. And he would deserve it. She was going to be so angry at him for not telling her and letting the situation get so bad. They had always split the finances. But when they bought the house, they had just moved the payments into the accounts he managed and she had taken the household accounts to run.

Even though she had quit her job a year ago at a major supply office to study for the real estate license exam and just hadn't taken it yet, he still loved her more than he wanted to think about. He didn't know what she did all day while he was job searching, but that didn't stop his love for her.

After two coffee shops today, he had finally gained a backbone. It was only two in the afternoon and he was headed home to finally tell her the problem.

Maybe together they could get through this because he was having no luck on his own. The debts were just too much.

He had never gone home in the middle of the afternoon before. Never.

His schedule was very regulated in his old job and Pam knew that.

The subdivision looked awfully quiet at this time of the day.

Every house in this area of the subdivision had been built off of five basic models, all two stories tall with wood shingles. All paint colors and any kind of landscaping had to be approved by the homeowners association from a very narrow list. The paints were all soft blues, tans, and greens. Very soft.

Boring soft.

Amazing how seeing a neighborhood in the cold light of financial ruin could make it look so different.

And he hated the beavers even more now.

But Pam loved the house and the entire neighborhood and she thought the beavers cute. To Neil the entire place felt more and more every day like a jail cell, with rows of metal beavers as his jailers.

Finally, after almost three months, on this beautiful spring day, he had decided to tell her. They were now over two months behind on their mortgage and about to fall into foreclosure. And he had maxed their credit cards on gas and other things for the house.

He had no choice. He would have to take the risk of losing her.

And losing all the rows of beavers as well.

He would miss Pam with all his heart if she left him. And he wouldn't blame her if she did. He had made a horrid and stupid blunder.

But he wouldn't miss the beavers.

TWO

AS HE HEADED down the street toward his home, he noticed three For Sale signs on lawns. And numbers of other houses looked empty.

One had a bank foreclosure sign on it.

Clearly he wasn't the only one in beaver land to be having problems.

There were very few cars in the driveways along the street since most of the homeowners were off at work and at this time of the day in the spring, the kids were all still in school. Luckily, he and Pam had no kids.

A blue Mercedes sedan sat in front of his house as he pulled into the driveway. Suddenly his mind spun out of control.

Was Pam having an affair on him?

When he asked her what she did all day, she had always avoided the question with just "Worked around the house."

Of course, when she asked him how the job was going, he just had avoided the question like she had.

It seemed their marriage had been built on distrust for some time now. How had it gotten down to that? At one point they had been the power couple among their friends, the two that would take over the world.

Now they couldn't even make a mortgage payment.

Or tell each other the truth.

He pulled into the driveway and instead of hitting the garage door opener, he just parked and got out into the warm afternoon air and closed his car door quietly.

He could smell the scent of freshly mowed grass and in the distance he could hear a leaf blower.

With his key in hand, he went to the front door and quietly opened it and stepped inside.

Pam's laugh came from the kitchen.

He loved her laugh, but at this moment, hearing that laugh, he almost turned and left. He didn't want to confront what he might see if he went around that corner into the dining room.

Just as he hadn't wanted to confront Pam when he lost his job.

It seems he was a coward, a lot more than he had ever thought of himself as one before.

When had he become so afraid?

He took a deep breath and stepped into the dining area that was beside the large, modern kitchen that Pam loved so much. The house smelled of bacon, so she must have cooked herself a bacon and cheese sandwich for lunch. She loved those as well.

Pam's eyes actually brightened as she saw him and she smiled and stood up from where she sat across from a man in a blue casual shirt. Pam had on her tan slacks and a white blouse and tan jacket, with earrings. She looked like she had just come home from an office.

She came over and kissed him hard, then smiled and turned. "Neil, I want you to meet Karl Benson. Karl, this is my husband, Neil."

"I've heard a lot about you," Karl said, standing and moving to shake Neil's hand. "Great to finally meet you and get you on board all this."

Neil shook his hand, putting on his company face, the one that tried not to show his complete bafflement at the situation.

On the counter where Karl and Pam had sat were folders and a lot of papers.

"What are you two up to?" Neil asked, nodding at the papers.

"Just some work I've been meaning to tell you about," Pam said, smiling at Karl and moving back to the counter.

She gathered up a few of the papers, then looked up at Karl. "Mind if I keep these for the evening and show Neil?"

"Not at all," Karl said. "See you at the Morrison property around ten tomorrow morning?"

"Sounds perfect," Pam said. "We'll be there."

Karl turned to Neil and smiled. "Wonderful to finally put a face to the name. See you tomorrow."

And with that, he headed out.

Neil watched him go, then turned back to Pam who had finished straightening up the piles of papers and had them stacked in neat, clearly labeled folders.

"So what's going on?" Neil asked.

"I'll explain it all in a minute, but first I want to know if you found a job? Is that why you are home early?"

Neil sort of rocked back. "You knew?"

She laughed and came over and kissed him. "Of course I knew and I also knew how hard you were looking for a new one. It was boneheaded for you to keep it from me, but I loved you for trying to protect me like that. Very macho in a 1950s sitcom fashion."

He laughed, letting the feeling of relief spread through his body. "Stupid was what it was."

"Note that you said that and I didn't disagree," she said. "So, did you find a job?"

"Nothing," he said. "It's as dry as a bone out there. I came home to finally tell you."

"Good," she said, smiling and kissing him again.

"Good?" he asked. "It's not good at all. We're about to drop into foreclosure."

"I know," she said. "It won't happen, but I knew."

"How did you know?" he asked, again stunned. "And why won't it happen?"

"Because I am basically rich beyond both our wildest expectations," she said, motioning him to come and join her at the counter. "And that's why I'm glad you didn't find a job because I need you working with me on this now."

"On what?" he asked, feeling more stunned than he had felt in years. He had come home expecting to maybe lose Pam for being so stupid in not telling her about his job. None of what she was saying was making sense.

"I decided I wouldn't tell you what I was doing until you got up the nerve to tell me about the job loss," she said.

"Sorry about that again," he said, his fear again coming back. "I honestly thought I could find another one in a week and not worry about it."

"And then a week turned into a month and then two months, right?" she asked.

"It was killing me," he said. "I didn't want you to think of me as a loser who couldn't even keep a job."

"Pride can make a person really stupid at times," she said, smiling at him.

He could only nod. She wasn't furious, but he could also tell he was a long ways from hearing the end of his idiotic blunder.

"So why are you rich and who exactly is Karl?"

"Karl is one of my bankers," she said. "He's handling the different trusts for me from his bank side."

"You have bankers?" Neil asked. "And trusts?"

"Let me start from the beginning," she said, laughing. "I learned about your job loss about a week after it happened and let me tell you, I was pissed you hadn't told me."

"You had a right to be," he said.

"But that week my Aunt Kelli died and I got distracted."

"You didn't tell me," he said, his voice sounding hollow to his own ears.

"Do you blame me?"

"Not in the slightest."

And he didn't.

"Did I miss her funeral?"

"She didn't have one," Pam said. "Otherwise I would have told you about that."

He nodded. "I'm sorry she's gone. She was a nice person."

"I miss her as well," Pam said. "But we really weren't that close. I just was the only sane one in her family that wasn't after her money, so she gave most of it to me."

"You're kidding? She had money?"

Pam just smiled. "It turned out Aunt Kelli was very rich and I was pretty much her only heir. She mostly cut off her two kids and had already transferred most everything she owned to me in different trusts which became mine at her death."

"How rich was she?" he asked, almost afraid of the answer.

He had liked Aunt Kelli and had been able to make her laugh at times, but he really didn't know that much about her and she had lived in an older home that

needed repairs she kept saying she would get around to.

"You know the building you used to work in?" Pam said.

He nodded. It was a seven-story office building in a nice area of town. Modern and expensive.

"It's in one of my trusts. I own it outright, among many other businesses, a small mall, and more apartment buildings than Karl and I can count."

All Neil could do was stare at his wife, his mouth open.

He must still be back in the coffee shop, dreaming. And if he was, he sure didn't want to wake up.

THREE

THE NEXT DAY Pam paid off the entire house mortgage and all the credit cards, erasing in a few phone calls two months of his worry. They went out to dinner to celebrate no debt and being very, very rich.

And the meal was wonderful. They splurged on lobster and the most expensive place in town. It had felt wonderful.

But over the next week it became clear to him very quickly how things were going to be going forward.

He had found a new job. It was working for Pam and the trusts.

It was not their money. It was her money.

She ran the trusts.

She controlled the money.

She just needed him to help her.

The job was right up his alley, actually. He reported to Pam and bossed around a lot of people under him. He managed property and he had an office beside Pam on the top floor of one of her buildings.

But she constantly made it clear that the money was hers, not his.

And he never said a word.

She knew he was a coward and never would say anything.

He had failed, both as a husband in not telling her about his job loss for months and as a business person in not finding a job on his own.

He had proven in a very clear fashion to her that he was a loser. He was useful and she still loved him, but he would never be her real partner in anything again.

Sure, they acted like a married couple and even slept in the same bed and had great sex and laughed and enjoyed each other's company.

He was good for that much at least.

But on the drive home, often alone, he knew the truth.

He had lied to her for months and she had the money and now she was running things.

Period.

And every morning and every evening, driving past those metal beavers on all the mailboxes, he swore they were sneering at him for being such a coward.

For being so stupid.

For being such a loser.

And if they were sneering at him, they were right.

He had made his choice.

He had compromised his last bit of dignity for money and to live in the land of metal beavers.

He deserved whatever look they gave him.

FOUR

IT TOOK JUST under three years before Neil finally had enough.

The day was like any other, warm outside, summer promising soon.

Pam had come into his office, treating him like a secretary, asking why something wasn't done yet.

He had been getting more and more tired of living in her shadow, of feeling worthless. Of all the bosses he had had over the years, she was by far the worst.

By far.

And he had to go home with her every night.

Their marriage was nothing more than a sham and they both knew it. But they never talked about it, just as he had never brought up the fact that he didn't feel like an equal in their marriage.

That's because he wasn't.

And they both knew that as well.

This was her business. He just worked for her.

So after she stood there in the doorway demanding he do something that seemed far, far below his level, he finally clicked over.

The proverbial straw.

He let out a deep sigh and could feel his resolve finally become action and movement.

"I'm going to go home for a time," he said, closing his desk and standing. "I don't feel well."

That stopped her in her tracks. He had never been sick a day in his life and for a moment he actually caught at flash of worry on her face.

"What's wrong?" she asked.

He looked up at her and shook his head. "Somewhere in the last four years I seem to have misplaced my courage, my ability to stand up for myself, my feeling of being worth something. I'm going to go see if I can find it."

He walked around his desk and directly at her where she stood in the door. "Good luck with all this. You should be able to find another flunky easy enough."

He kissed her on the forehead and then pushed past, heading across the reception area for the elevator.

"What are you doing?" she demanded, acting as if she was still in charge of him.

"As I said, I'm going home for a short time to pack a few things."

"You are leaving me?"

She sounded stunned.

"Of course I am," he said, punching the elevator button and then looking back at her angry and surprised look. "What did you expect? I was a man when you married me. Sure, I made a big mistake when I lost my last job, but working like this as your flunky for years is more punishment than I can take."

She stood there, her anger turning to a stunned look on her beautiful face. Clearly she had never thought this day would come. That's how little respect she had for him.

Wow, that was sad.

He really had gotten that pathetic.

"I still love you, Pam," he said as the elevator door slid open and he stepped on. "Enjoy your money. I'll be out of the way by the time you get home."

She said nothing as the elevator doors closed and he turned off his cell phone before he reached the ground floor.

It took him only twenty minutes to pack and fill the back of his paid-off SUV with his stuff. And in the back of his closet he found his guitar. When he pulled it out, his mood soured.

He had stuffed who he really was away for far too long.

She did not show up.

She really didn't think he would go through with this, did she?

He looked at the house, then down the quiet suburban street at the rows of houses that all looked the same and the rows of metal beavers on every mailbox.

God, he had come to hate this place.

But mostly he had come to hate himself.

There was a baseball bat lying on the neighbor's lawn and he went over and picked it up. It felt good in his hands.

Real good.

He moved back over to his mailbox, then with one swing, he smashed the beaver from the top of the box. It went sailing out into the street, the sound echoing down the quiet street.

A surge of excitement went through him, something he hadn't felt in years.

He climbed into the SUV with the bat. His guitar was on the seat beside him.

He rolled down his driver's window.

Then he backed out into the street and gave his house one more look, just as he had given Pam one more look.

Pam would sure be shocked when she got home and he wasn't here waiting for her. She had grown very used to being in charge. This would hurt her ego more than anything.

Then, laughing a real laugh for the first time in years, he turned and headed out of the subdivision, smashing the smirk off of every beaver as he passed.

~

USA *Today* Bestselling Writer

DEAN WESLEY SMITH

A MATTER FOR A FUTURE YEAR

A Seeders Universe Story

A single Seeder scout ship trapped on the edge of a distant, uncharted galaxy. Chairman Peter German holds the fate of the three thousand people on the Pale Light.

Main drives mysteriously not working, the ship hobbles along at sub-light speed with not enough supplies to reach the nearest Earth-like planet.

The Chairman faces a hard, hard choice. He must find the solution.

Galaxy spanning ships, billions of civilizations, the Seeders Universe stories and novels cover it all. But "A Matter for a Future Year" brings it all down to a single human choice. And the price paid by those who risk to explore outward.

A MATTER FOR A FUTURE YEAR
A Seeders Universe Story

ONE

"IT'S NOT GOING to work," Davis said, staring at the control panel in front of him.

The silence in the massive control room felt like a weight on Chairman Peter German, pressing down on his chest. Twenty officers still pretended to study their stations, but all of them were waiting for his response. He knew that.

He glanced at Davis, his best friend and third in command. Davis was bald and liked to wear T-shirts. Davis only shrugged an apology at the answer.

German could sense the growing frustration, anger, and even hints of panic in his command bridge crew. He felt the same emotions exactly.

German stood six feet tall, had striking black hair that trailed over his collar, and dark green eyes that people said felt like he could look through them. No one had ever questioned his ability to lead and no one was now either. In fact, they were depending on his leadership.

He wore tan slacks, an open-neck dress shirt, and tennis shoes. After centuries on this ship, uniforms were a forgotten thing of the past for everyone.

In situations like this, he never sat down, but instead either stood by his own chair so he could see his panels, or roamed around the bridge.

In his seven hundred years of being a Chairman of the Seeder's scout ship *Pale Light*, he had never felt so bad, so lost, or so flat confused as he did right now. But he sure couldn't show that or admit that to his bridge crew. Over eighty thousand people on this ship depended on him and his bridge crew to find a solution.

So they would find one.

Pale Light and everyone on board had all made a great living for centuries. All Seeder ships ran like a corporation, which was why he was called Chairman. On top of that, he had gotten the original

funding for the ship and had the most shares in the corporation. Over the centuries, they had taken many lucrative contracts to scout galaxies ahead of the wave of Seeder ships.

At the moment they were twenty galaxies out ahead of the front wave. It would take the front wave of Seeder ships over two hundred thousand years to work their way here, and that was because most of the galaxies between here and the main wave were small.

Pale Light, with him in charge, had explored uncounted galaxies, had even discovered two young alien races in different galaxies and seen remnants of three other alien races in three other galaxies. Everyone on board got bonuses when they found aliens and warned the Seeder ships in the main wave away from those galaxies.

Now *Pale Light* had a problem.

Everyone on board had a problem.

They were dead in space. And not a person on the ship had any idea why or what was wrong.

They had suddenly dropped out of drive at a dead stop. That should not have been possible either, but it had happened.

And unless they solved this problem in short order, he would have to start putting most of the people on board into suspended animation, something that had never been done on *Pale Light* since it was built.

He had already given the order to start checking the chambers and preparing them.

Pale Light just didn't have enough supplies on board to feed all eighty thousand people for the five-year sub-light trip to the nearest inhabitable planet.

And even when they got there, they would be stuck on a single planet in a galaxy with nothing more than a number designation and no hope of anyone even looking for them for two or three hundred years.

He could smell the sweat of the officers around him, many who had served with him for centuries. They all knew that scouting into other galaxies was a dangerous mission. Many Seeder scout ships like the *Pale Light* had gone missing over the centuries. That's why they had been paid so well. But after centuries, he had forgotten the danger.

They all had.

Now the reason they had been paid so much faced them.

He glanced around at his top bridge crew. All of them needed a break from the bridge, him included. They had been working on what had happened and different solutions to what was wrong with *Pale Light* and the future that faced them for over five hours straight.

There had to be a solution, a reason for the sudden stop. But none of them could find it yet.

Pale Light should be working fine. It was not.

It was that simple.

The reason why was the main problem as far as he was concerned.

And the second problem was what to do about it.

And about the eighty thousand people who worked for him.

They had less than twenty-four hours by everyone's calculation before he would have to order most of the population of *Pale Light* into the suspension chambers to give a skeleton crew enough supplies to make it the five years of sub-light travel.

He did not want to do that because he understood, just as everyone on this bridge understood, that just under one percent of the humans going into suspended animation did not wake up.

That meant that the moment he gave that order, he was sentencing a lot of people who worked for him to their death.

But if he didn't order it, they would all starve in a matter of months.

He ran his fingers through his black hair, then took a deep breath and said to the bridge crew. "We get some food, some showers, mandatory for all of us, and some rest. We return here in six hours, rested, cleaned up and ready to solve this. Get the evening crew to take over until then."

With that, German teleported to his cabin.

He loved his four-room suite. He had decorated the rooms in soft browns, with soft brown furniture, warm, comfortable tan floors, and wood-toned tables and countertops.

His fiancée, Dr. Kathy Spears, had helped him. A couple times he had tried to get her to join him on the *Pale Light*, but she had wanted to stay in her practice for a few more years.

They talked almost every night and since *Pale Light* reported back every two years, they reconnected then and spent six months together. One of these times, she would join him. She had promised. But as she said, they had lots of time.

He picked up the holo-image of Kathy on his bedroom nightstand, then put it back down again.

He couldn't think about her right now and he didn't dare allow himself to even think about the problem. He needed some rest. He stripped off his clothes and climbed into his shower. Ten minutes later, feeling slightly refreshed, he put on fresh clothes and went into his kitchen to fix himself a sandwich.

After eating half the turkey sandwich and drinking a glass of fruit juice, he was ready for a nap.

There was a solution. He knew that. They just had to find it.

And find out why this had happened in the first place.

Rest would help.

He cleared his mind, lay down on the bed, and was asleep almost instantly.

Centuries of practice clearing ship's business from his mind before sleeping allowed him to do that.

Even dire problems.

TWO

CHAIRMAN PETER GERMAN woke three hours later, feeling much better.

He washed off his face, once again changed to a clean shirt, and went back to the kitchen to finish the other half of the turkey sandwich he had made earlier.

As he ate, he pulled up some of the data they had worked out earlier.

If a support crew was going to have enough food to survive a five-year sub-light trip to the nearest planet that would sustain a human population, he had to order all but three hundred of the eighty thousand on board into suspended animation. They would lose around five hundred people if he did that, but the rest would survive.

Sub-light drives worked, but something had blocked the *Pale Light's* hyper drives. Everything showed fine on all engine readings, just something stopped the ship from jumping.

It was as if hyper space, real space, and everything else around them had just stopped existing.

They had done every reading of the empty space around them that they could and some that no one had even tried in centuries. Nothing was there.

Nothing.

Empty space surrounded them.

But he and all the scientists on board knew that empty space, really, truly empty space did not exist. Space was always full of so many things. But it seemed empty space actually did exist and they were parked solidly in the middle of a large bubble of it.

With that, he went to his private research computer in his office. That computer gave him access to many confidential reports in the Seeder's network and command structure that had been stored on board and updated every time they returned to the leading edge with their reports. He was the only one on board that had access to the confidential files, although if something happened to him, Rose Marie, his second in command, knew where they were and how to get into them.

He looked up the reference to "empty space" to see if other ships had run into this kind of thing before.

What he found scared him more than the idea of putting almost everyone who worked for him into suspended animation.

It seemed that major studies, all highly classified, had been done on Empty Space or Void Space as it was called. It seemed that nothing existed in the space, including time.

Empty Space was basically a void in time and space. The voids were small and no one in his main records had figured out how they were formed. But it had a very real warning. If caught by one, get out quickly.

Another scientist called Empty Space the only reliable time travel machine into the future in the universe.

"Oh, shit," German said, his stomach twisting down on the turkey sandwich he had just finished.

He touched a button on his wall. "All command crew return at once to the bridge."

He instantly teleported there.

A young man by the name of Moore was at the helm. He had a head of bright red hair and freckles. He usually only saw duty in the night shift.

"Moore," German said, "ease sub-light drive up to full at once."

Moore nodded and focused on his panel.

German turned to his second in command, Rose Marie, who had just appeared on the bridge. Her short brown hair was still wet and she looked as if she had missed a button in getting her light blue blouse on in a rush.

"Head us toward that planet we found earlier that's five years out," German said

to her and she nodded and stepped to navigation.

German turned back to Moore. "We at full speed yet?"

"We are, sir," Moore said. "Eighty percent of light."

"Then push it harder."

"But…" Moore started to say.

German nodded. "I know all about time issues at sub-light. Just do it. I want this ship going at 95 percent of light speed as soon as you can get it worked up there. When we get out we'll reset all the clocks."

Moore only nodded and turned back to his controls.

Davis was now back at his panel, so German turned to his friend, "How far to the edge of Empty Space?"

"At 95 percent of light, we should get there in twenty-two hours."

German took a deep breath. That was a very, very long time.

Maybe too long.

"Davis, Rose Marie, I need you both in my cabin in ten minutes."

With that he jumped back to his cabin suite, got himself a glass of apricot juice, and dropped onto his couch in his living room. There was an image of Kathy on the end table.

He reached over and turned the image off.

He would let Rose Marie and Davis look at the classified files on the studies of Empty Space when they got here. And then they could talk about it.

And decide exactly what to do or not do.

But now he knew why Seeder Scout Ships vanished at times.

Empty Space.

They didn't vanish. They just took a trip into the future.

How far into the future was now the question.

THREE

CHAIRMAN PETER GERMAN stood beside Davis and watched the screens around the large bridge. So far nothing on long-range sensors had changed. The small galaxy they had been exploring when trapped by Empty Space had not changed at all.

"Ten seconds to the edge," Rose Marie said, moving over to stand on the other side of German from Davis.

They had no idea what would happen when they crossed over that edge.

Or if Empty Space would even let them leave. There just hadn't been enough data in those classified files to help them even begin to make an educated guess.

But German was betting that once outside the confines of the Empty Space bubble, *Pale Light* would work just fine. At least he hoped it would. Because if it didn't, he would have to order most of the employees on board into animation.

"Now!" Davis said as the *Pale Light* went through the edge of the Empty Space bubble.

Everything changed.

As German had feared, the universe they had left when they entered Empty Space was not the same universe they had returned to.

There were gasps from around the bridge.

"Not possible," one person said.

German wanted to say "Very possible." But didn't.

"Get us away from that thing a ways and slow us down," German said to navigation. His concern right now was not what had happened to the outside world, but to what was happening inside *Pale Light*.

Davis was ahead in the thought. He turned to engineering. "Are standard drives working?"

"They are," Flame said from his panel, almost bouncing in excitement.

"Jump us a few light years away from that Empty Space and come to full stop," German said. "Then I want reports."

But German knew what he was seeing on the screens. The galaxy they were in had already been seeded and was a good hundred thousand years into development.

The front wave of the Seeder Ships had gotten here and passed right by them.

They had been inside that small bubble for at least three hundred thousand years.

"Find the front line of the seeding ships," German said, turning to Rose Marie.

She nodded and went back to her station.

German stood there, just staring at the inhabited galaxy they had been scouting. He never went back into the galaxies after seeding. He knew that millions of Seeders stayed behind to guild the seeded human cultures up to maturity. But he had never been one of them.

He always liked being out ahead of the crowds.

Seeing a galaxy alive with human life just felt odd to him. Galaxies he explored never had anything more than lower animal life. If that.

Rose Marie came back and stood beside German and Davis as they both stared at the screens and the data and reports starting to pour in from all the stations around the ship.

"The front line is working about ten galaxies beyond this one," Rose Marie said. "About a four-month trip at normal speeds."

"We were in Empty Space for three hundred and twenty-one thousand years," Davis said. "The people on board with families back on the old front line are going to have problems."

German nodded. "Get the counseling services warned."

He didn't let himself think about Kathy.

Davis moved to get that started.

"So now what do we do?" Rose Marie asked, her voice almost a whisper, as if talking to herself.

"The same thing we have always done," German said without looking away from all the reports flowing in. "We go back to command, get paid, and get back to work."

"Think we have back pay waiting for us?" Davis asked as he rejoined them.

German laughed. "This might be a very rich ship by the time we go back out again."

"Three hundred thousand years of progress," Rose Marie said. "This ship might be very dated."

German shook his head. "I doubt it will be. Seeders don't invent new things very often. We just explore and keep moving forward and giving human life to every planet we can find."

"Ain't that the truth," Davis said.

German turned to Rose Marie. "Get us to command. We have some reports to file and back pay to collect."

She nodded and with that he teleported back to his suite. Then, with a quick search through the Seeder database, he discovered what had happened to Kathy.

Five years after he and *Pale Light* had vanished without a trace, she married another doctor.

Three hundred and ten years later, while on a rescue mission to a small moon, she died in a ship crash.

He went into his bedroom, took her holo-image cube from his nightstand, then went into the living room and took her picture from there and put both cubes in a drawer.

And as he closed the drawer over her, he said simply, "Sorry."

Then he squared his shoulders and teleported back to the bridge. He had a business to run, eighty thousand people on board to help get through this. He would grieve for Kathy later.

Much later.

He had a job to do first.

———

USA TODAY BESTSELLING AUTHOR

DEAN WESLEY SMITH

AN EASY SHOT

A GOLF THRILLER

Seattle detectives Craig and Bonnie Frakes wanted nothing more but to enjoy each other's company and their golf vacation in Scottsdale. They needed the rest.

Their vacation plans take a sudden turn when they overhear a conversation plotting a murder.

A fast-paced thriller that I first published years ago under another title and under a pen name. The publishing company died just as this book came out, so I figured it would be fun to bring the book back and give it a second life here.

AN EASY SHOT

For KKR, always the love of my life

PROLOGUE

Monday, April 3rd
11:12 p.m.

CHARLES ROBINS IGNORED the crisp desert air and the star-filled Arizona night as he stepped onto the stone patio of his Scottsdale mansion. His entire focus was on the dark-suited man who leaned against a rock wall, smoking.

Beyond the wall, the lights of Phoenix stretched out across the valley floor. Often, on spring nights like this, Charles would have his after-dinner brandy served on this patio. He loved the view, the lights, the feeling of being above all the masses below.

But not tonight.

At the moment there was much more important business to attend to. There would always be other warm nights and brandy on the patio.

The man dropped the red-tipped cigarette and ground it under his foot as Charles closed the patio door and turned.

The man would fit into most crowds. His dark suit wasn't expensive, but it wasn't cheap either. His face was clean shaven and had nothing really distinctive about it. His hair was short and he was going slightly bald. Charles doubted he would even recognize the man if they passed on the street. Yet the man was one of Charles's most trusted and valued employees.

The man waited, making Charles come to him. No one else could do that. Charles controlled businesses worth a billion dollars, had twenty servants and six body guards in this house alone, and was considered one of the most eligible bachelors in the country. Yet this man just didn't seem to care.

Charles asked him to do special tasks, paid him well, and that was all the man did. He scared Charles by his very coldness. No one else in this world did that to Charles.

In the three years the man had worked for Charles, this was only their fourth meeting. All four meetings had been on this patio, and always alone. Charles didn't even know the man's real name and had no desire to learn it. Charles just called him Bill when he had to call him anything at all, and the man didn't seem to care. Yet Charles knew to the penny how many hundreds of thousands of dollars this man, under a false company name, had been paid for "consulting."

And every penny had been worth it.

The man spoke little, and Charles liked that about him. Tonight there were no greetings. The man, his dark eyes hidden in the faint light, simply stood and waited, his hands behind his back, as if he were in control.

That attitude made Charles feel even less sure about what he was about to do, but at this point he could see no other choice.

"Senator Knight from California will be playing in a pro-am golf tournament here in Scottsdale this weekend," Charles said, keeping his voice low so that it wouldn't carry in the desert air. "Then he will be flying to Washington for a vote Monday morning."

The man said nothing.

Charles went on. "I want you to make sure he doesn't make that trip."

"Never make the trip?" the man asked, his voice very low and deep. "Or delayed?"

"I don't honestly care," Charles said. And he didn't. Senator Kelly had been after him for years. Having the man permanently out of the picture would not be a bad thing. But it was critical Kelly didn't make that vote.

"Understood," the man said, nodding once. "Is that all?"

"Make it look like an accident if you can," Charles said. "But if you can't just make sure it's done. He cannot be allowed to be in Washington on Monday. Understood?"

Again the man nodded once. "This is a United States Senator you are talking about. It will cost you more."

"Of course," Charles said. "Just get it done."

Without even a nod the man turned and started down the rock path beside the garage wall. The night seemed to swallow him. One moment there, the next gone. How the man got past Grant and his men, and in and out of the estate's security system was another question Charles just didn't want to know the answer to.

Charles stared after the man for a moment, feeling uncertain, and very worried, just as he had felt every other time he had talked to him. Yet the man always got the task done.

Charles turned to look out over the lights of the valley below. This mansion, all his property, everything he owned and controlled, was being threatened and he couldn't let that happen. Senator Kelly was the push behind legislation that would cripple two of Charles's main companies, and lead to investigations that Charles knew he couldn't withstand. If Senator Kelly's legislation passed, Charles would be broke and fighting to stay out of jail in less than a year.

Most of his waking hours—and many of his nightmares—over the last few months had been to fight this bill. He had wrapped up enough votes in Kelly's committee to tie and kill the bill if Kelly didn't vote. But Chairman Kelly's vote would put the bill on the floor of the Senate and from there it couldn't be stopped.

The key to it all was making sure Senator Kelly didn't make that vote.

Charles glanced down the dark path where the man he called Bill had disappeared. He could see nothing.

With a deep breath of the fresh, crisp night air, Charles turned and headed back inside. He had a lot of work to do and work was always the best thing to take his mind off of what he had just ordered done.

If that was even possible.

Friday, April 7th
8:02 a.m.

THE THREE GUNMEN walked into the small apartment of Steph and Danny Baines without knocking. Two wore masks, the third, who was in charge, didn't seem to care who saw him. But he knew that the residents of the nearby apartments had all left for work. Only twenty-four-year-old Steph Barnes was at home.

The small apartment hugged against the back of a large red rock just above the small valley that held Sedona, Arizona. It had one bedroom, a small living room and kitchen, and a fantastic view of the red-rock country around Sedona from a balcony.

Danny worked as the assistant golf pro for the local country club and Steph taught sixth grade. They were both from Phoenix, had met in college, and were hoping that Danny would get a job this next fall on one of the bigger Scottsdale clubs so they could move back. They both loved Sedona, but it was just too cold in the winter for both of them.

Danny stood just under six feet tall, had sun-bleached brown hair and a smooth-as-silk golf swing. Steph was almost as tall, with light auburn hair and a smile that could melt a sixth-grader. Everyone said they looked more like brother and sister than husband and wife.

Steph had taken the morning off from school to help Danny get ready for the charity tournament in Phoenix. They both had figured that it would be a wonderful opportunity to meet some people who might help them get back into the Phoenix area. And when he learned he was playing with Senator Knight, Danny got even more excited. Steph was going to come down by bus on Saturday and join the group on Sunday. Not only was it going to be a good chance for Danny to make contacts, it was going to be fun as well.

Steph had just dropped a fifth golf shirt into Danny's suitcase when the front door opened. For a moment she thought it was Danny coming back from the course early. Then she heard a strange voice from the doorway.

"Don't scream or nothin'" the voice said. "Just finish packin' for your husband and everything will be just fine."

She spun around to face three men. All were holding machine-gun-like weapons on her.

Somehow she managed to not scream. Somehow.

CHAPTER ONE

Friday, April 7th
9:20 p.m.

THE WARM DESERT breeze wrapped around Craig Frakes as he stopped to look back up the hill at the lights of the Canyon Hotel nestled into the rocks. After the long winter in Seattle, he couldn't believe he was here in Scottsdale, Arizona, getting ready to play an entire weekend of golf. This had to be a dream. He was sure he would wake up any moment to the sound of rain pounding against the bedroom window.

His wife, Bonnie, stopped beside him and took his hand, also staring up at the resort they were staying in for the next three nights. "Beautiful, isn't it?"

Beautiful didn't really begin to describe it. The Canyon Hotel had been built using the massive brown rocks and the desert hillside as a frame. The architect had nestled the rooms into the canyon walls, mixing large timbers and massive boulders throughout. The main area was a combination of stone, wood, and soft carpets that felt more like a warm cave and a living room than a hotel lobby.

And the fantastic architecture didn't stop at the lobby. Their room—as the hotel called it—was more like a suite, with a light brown leather couch and chair, a massive bed, and a bathroom larger than some apartments he had rented in college. A switch inside the bathroom door sent a waterfall cascading over rocks and down into a large tub. Craig couldn't imagine how every room in the hotel could be as plush as theirs, but he had a hunch every room was.

From where they stood on the path near the first tee of the Canyon Resort Golf Club, the hotel lights filled the night with a soft glow that felt welcoming and warm, barely pushing back the light from the stars and the small crescent moon.

"You know what's really great about being here?" he asked, looking over at his beautiful wife. Her hair seemed to shimmer in the glow from the hotel and she looked almost waif-like in the white shorts and light blouse.

"What?" she asked, smiling at him.

"It's warm," he said, "it's not raining, and my lips are already chapping from the dryness. What more can a guy ask for?"

She laughed, the sound carrying out over the open fairway and lush grass. "Oh, I can think of a few more things."

She squeezed his hand and pulled him away from staring at the hotel and down the dark, paved golf path that led along the right side of the first hole of the course. "Come on, let's go for a walk."

Now that she mentioned it, Craig could think of a few other things he *could* ask for. And knowing Bonnie, he just might be lucky enough tonight to get one of those wishes.

"Going to be tough to see what the golf course is like in the dark," he said.

"I wasn't thinking of looking at the golf course," she said.

"Oh, I like the sound of that," he said, as they topped over a small rise and headed down a shallow hill that slowly blocked the lights of the hotel.

After the last six months of hard work, they had been looking forward to this vacation. They both worked for the Seattle police department. He was a homicide detective, while she had moved off the streets and now worked special services dealing in domestic violence and runaway children.

Everyone said they made the perfect couple. He was six-one and had just turned thirty-one. She was five-two and thirty. Both of them had dark brown hair, but Bonnie's eyes were a deep brown while his were green.

They had met in college and lived together for years before finally getting married. At some point they both wanted children, but so far their jobs kept them too busy.

He stayed in shape by running and lifting weights, while Bonnie liked swimming more. But they were both avid golfers. Bonnie's handicap was three shots lower than Craig's, and she beat him three out of their four outings, something Craig very seldom let her forget. They loved the game and the good-natured rivalry, and when the opportunity to represent the Seattle Police Department in this charity golf tournament came along, they jumped at the chance to get out of the Seattle spring weather and actually play a round of golf without wearing rain gear.

On top of that, this weekend was going to be the first real vacation they had had in over a year. Craig couldn't believe it had been that long. Being a detective never seemed to allow for much free time. And Bonnie's job wasn't any better. At one point earlier this spring she had had over one hundred active cases of children needing homes, abused spouses, and missing children. He marveled at her strength under that heavy a load.

Now here they were, walking on what seemed to be a perfect-temperature evening in Arizona, the cares of police work a long plane ride behind them.

"You're sure being quiet," Bonnie said as they strolled along the dark path, hand in hand.

They were walking slower than he remembered walking in a long time. It felt great. He could feel the tension draining from his back and shoulders.

"Just relaxing and watching the lights of the valley. And enjoying the company."

"How about enjoying the company a little more closely?" she asked, her voice low and sultry and very suggestive. She pulled him and they bumped hips.

Craig could barely see her smile in the dim light. She was teasing him and he was enjoying it.

"This far from the hotel room?" he asked, teasing back. "I'm afraid I just don't know what you have in mind?"

She laughed. "Six years of marriage and you've forgotten what we used to do on the muni course?"

He would never forget those nights, but instead he said, "Hmmm, how about a reminder?"

As the path crested a small rise near a massive boulder, she pulled him off the pavement and around the rock that towered over the edge of the fairway.

The grass on the other side was lush and soft as she pulled him down beside her. He expected it to be damp and cold, like the grass in the Pacific Northwest always was at night, but instead the fairway was dry and slightly warm from the heat of the day. He was starting to like the desert more and more.

The lights from the valley below gave them just enough light to see what they were doing, yet not enough for Craig to worry about being seen from any distance. And the boulder blocked the view to the path.

"This feels wonderful," Bonnie said, rubbing her hands over the ground as she kicked off her shoes.

"I couldn't agree more," he said, wrapping his arms around her and pulling her close for a long, passionate kiss.

His heart was racing and he was short of breath. For some reason he felt too old to be kissing out under the stars. That seemed like a young person's thing. When had he gotten so old?

He pushed the thought away and let the excitement of the moment take him. After a moment, he started to unbutton her blouse, slowly, carefully, not breaking the kiss.

He could feel her skin under his fingers, getting him even more excited than he already was. But he forced himself to try to take his time. In this kind of situation, that was going to be difficult, at best. It had been a long time since they had done something like this.

Too long.

Finally, after what seemed like an eternity of bumbling, he got the last button undone. It felt like a victory, the same as it had with his first girlfriend back in high school.

Bonnie pulled back. "I see you are remembering just fine."

He ran his hand over her breast, enjoying the soft feel of her skin and the silky feel of the bra. She shivered slightly and leaned into his touch.

"I think it's coming back to me," he said, "but I'm still not sure."

She laughed. "Let's be sure."

She pulled off her blouse and tossed it toward the base of the rock, then as he watched, she lay back, lifted her hips, and slipped off her white shorts, tossing them on top of the blouse.

Just the movement of her body in the faint light made him excited.

And the fear of getting caught. That was exciting him even more.

He glanced around, trying to listen *over* the sounds of his beating heart to see if anyone was coming. As far as he could tell, they were alone.

At least for the moment.

"No grass stains this time," she said.

He laughed. Back on one of their early college dates, they had ended up on the golf course, kissing and touching and having a great time late one night. Bonnie had been wearing white shorts like the ones she had just taken off, and they had gotten ruined from grass stains. And since she had been living at home at the time, it had been very embarrassing to explain to her mother.

"You got to admit, getting those grass stains was fun."

"And this isn't?" she asked, smiling.

"I didn't say that."

They kissed, long and hard, a kiss like they hadn't done in some time. Work had just been so much for both of them that sex had often taken a back seat. His hope, and it seemed to be Bonnie's as well, was that this weekend that would change. Sex would become something they focused on and enjoyed. And this was getting the weekend off to a great start as far as he was concerned.

In the faint light, she was fantastically beautiful. The white of her bra and thin panties was like a light beckoning him to come closer. And he obeyed.

Hell, he *wanted* to obey.

He let his hands brush up her legs, over her flat stomach, to her breasts.

She pulled back. "Wait just a minute. You have too many clothes on now."

With that she sat up and pulled on the bottom of his shirt, helping him take it over his head. It ended up in the pile with her clothes. Then she worked at his belt and unzipped his slacks as he took off his shoes.

He lay back, his butt off the ground, as in one smooth motion she pulled his pants off, leaving him laying in the middle of a fairway on the warm grass in only his white underwear.

It was the most excited he could remember feeling since college.

And the most afraid of getting caught.

He had forgotten what that feeling of doing something illegal was like.

The grass was warm and soft against his skin as he ran his hands over it. What the hell. If they got caught, they got caught. It was their vacation, after all. And they were a long way from home.

"Now you have too many clothes," he said.

"Oh, I like this game," she said, giving him a kiss and then pulling away.

As he watched, she unhooked her bra, tossing it aside with the rest of their

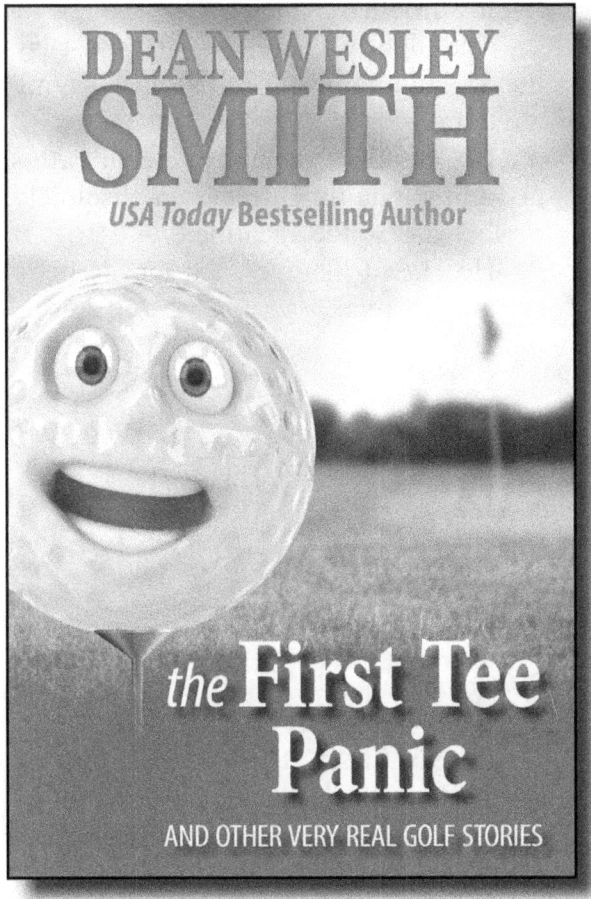

clothes. The soft light made her skin seem ultra smooth and silky, as if there wasn't a mole or wrinkle anywhere.

"Like what you see?" she asked, looking down at him.

"Much more than like," he said. "How about love? Admire? Adore?"

"You say all the right things," she said, her laugh carrying into the darkness of the desert and golf course. She lay on top of him. The feel of her breasts against his chest was wonderful.

"Nice," she said, pressing her leg into the hardness of his crotch.

He pulled her tight and they kissed again, moving their bodies slowly against each other. He wanted to touch, to stroke every inch of her. He loved the way she felt against him, her soft skin moving slowly against his.

He kept at it until she finally pulled his head up and kissed him long and hard.

He returned the kiss, suddenly not caring if anyone else was nearby or not. She rolled him over on his back and kneeling beside his legs pulled off his underwear with a frantic jerk, flicking them into the air over her head.

"Oh, I like this," she said, running her hands over him.

"You're not the only one," he said. The sensation was wonderful and much more intense than it had been in a long time.

The warm night, the fear of someone nearby, the grass against his back all seemed to vanish as his body pushed upward. Before she was all the way into position he couldn't help himself and started to move up and down under her.

After a wonderful eternity, they lay panting, sweating, both trying to catch what air they could manage.

That had been intense, and wonderful.

He kissed her neck and she shivered. But she didn't move.

He kissed it again and got the same reaction. Only this time she hugged him, being careful to keep him in the same position.

"Wow," he managed to whisper into her ear.

She squeezed him with her entire body. "Yeah. No argument there."

She carefully stretched out her legs and lay down on him, keeping them together as they rolled over so they were facing each other in a full hug. On one side he could feel her soft skin the length of his body, and on his back grass was sticking to his sweaty body.

With the stars above and warm night air around them, it was a moment he didn't want to let go of.

Clearly Bonnie didn't either.

There was no sound of anyone walking toward them.

The night was quiet, so they just lay there, holding each other, not saying anything.

He couldn't remember feeling this good in a long time. It was an absolutely perfect start to the vacation.

He closed his eyes and let his body completely relax.

CHAPTER TWO

Friday, April 7th
9:46 p.m.

DANNY BAINES TOSSED his bag on the hotel bed and looked around. In all his life he had never felt so scared, so alone, so completely out of his mind.

This all had to be a nightmare and he would wake up very shortly.

He walked into the large bathroom and stared in the mirror.

His eyes were red and he looked like he hadn't slept.

Actually he'd had a good night's sleep last night with Steph and this morning had headed to the course to get his clubs and help get ready for the weekend rush of players before he had to leave for Phoenix.

When he got home, he found his bag packed and sitting by the front door. A man he didn't recognize was sitting on the couch, pointing a gun at him.

Steph was nowhere to be found.

He almost went crazy when the guy said they had taken Steph. He stormed at the guy.

"If I shoot you," the guy had said, pointing the gun at Danny, "I have to kill your wife as well."

That stopped Danny.

And then Danny's blood seemed to freeze as the man laughed. "And she's a looker, too. It would be fun doin' her."

"So why are you doing this?" Danny had asked.

For the next twenty minutes the man had explained exactly why they had taken Steph. And what they wanted him to do to get her back.

Then the man had helped him carry his bag to his car, helped him check the apartment to make sure everything was turned off, and then stood there and watched Danny drive away.

Now Danny was in Phoenix, checked into his room, and going crazy. He couldn't do what they were asking.

He just couldn't.

But it seemed he had no choice.

He headed through the bedroom and out into the main area of the small suite.

The phone was sitting on the desk under a mirror. He moved over to it. He had to call the police. He had to have help.

He picked up the phone, then put it back down, the man's voice echoing in his ears. "Trust me," the man had said, "you call the police and we can kill your wife before you hang up the phone."

Those words echoed through his mind. How would they know if he called the police?

He couldn't take the chance.

The image of Steph's face filled his mind and he moved over to the couch and sat down.

It was going to be a very long night.

And an even longer golf tournament.

CHAPTER THREE

Friday, April 7th
9:53 p.m.

BONNIE'S BREATH WAS even against his neck, the grass soft under him, and he wasn't sure if he hadn't even dozed a little. Amazing, falling asleep nude in the middle of a fairway. This just wasn't like him at all.

Suddenly he realized what had woken him up.

Someone was coming!

The sound of a deep, male voice in the distance drifted over them.

He pulled back enough to see his wife's face in the dim light. Her eyes were closed and she seemed to be asleep as well. He could feel their skin sticking together.

He leaned in close to her ear. "I think someone's coming," he whispered, trying not to startle her.

"Oh, damn," she whispered back.

Her eyes snapped open and she rolled away from him.

The stickiness on his stomach had dried his skin against hers and it pulled like removing a bandage.

"How long were we asleep?" she whispered as she grabbed her shoes and the pile of clothes and moved over toward the side of the giant boulder that towered over them and the fairway. If they stayed against the backside of it, they wouldn't be seen from the cart path.

He grabbed his shoes and followed her as again the male voice could clearly be heard. At least two people were coming from the direction of the clubhouse, walking along the same path they had walked.

Bonnie, her back against the tall rock, slipped on her underwear, then shorts. He started to do the same, then realized his underwear was still out in the middle of the fairway where Bonnie had tossed them aside.

He eased away from the rock slightly and glanced toward the clubhouse. The silhouettes of two men could be seen coming up the small rise about a hundred yards away. One was smoking a cigarette and the red tip glowed in the dark.

"Shit!" he said, softly.

Craig pointed at his underwear and Bonnie snickered. If he went back out onto the fairway to get his underwear, he would be seen, so he slipped his pants on without them.

"Watch that zipper," Bonnie whispered as she put on her bra. "I don't want that part hurt."

"Trust me," he whispered back, "neither do I."

She laughed softly and they both sat down with their backs against the rock, waiting for the intruders to pass as they put on their shoes. He felt like a kid again, almost getting caught at something he shouldn't have been doing. His heart was beating hard and he was enjoying the feeling as the two men moved toward them.

This was fun.

And for some reason damn scary at the same time.

The sound of their footsteps seemed very loud, echoing over the grass and desert like irregular drum beats. Neither man had said a word for at least fifty paces. Then one with a high voice and a slight New York accent said, "I still can't believe we're doin' a Senator."

"Believe it," the other man said.

The second man had a deep, distinctive voice that sounded like a musician's.

"I don't much like the idea of the entire fucking government comin' after me."

The two men were even with the rock and passing.

Craig glanced at Bonnie. Her eyes were huge and she was holding her breath just as he was. Suddenly this had turned from fun to something very serious.

"If nothing goes wrong, no one will be coming after you," the deep-voiced one said. "We just make sure it looks like an accident."

"Yeah, sure," the first man said as the two started down the hill away from Bonnie and Craig. "I better be gettin' paid real good for this."

"Trust me," the deep-voiced man said, "you are. We all are."

"We better," the man said. "A senator. This is nuts."

Craig stared at Bonnie as the two men moved on, clearly headed somewhere out

Now Available
from all your favorite booksellers
in trade paper and electronic editions.

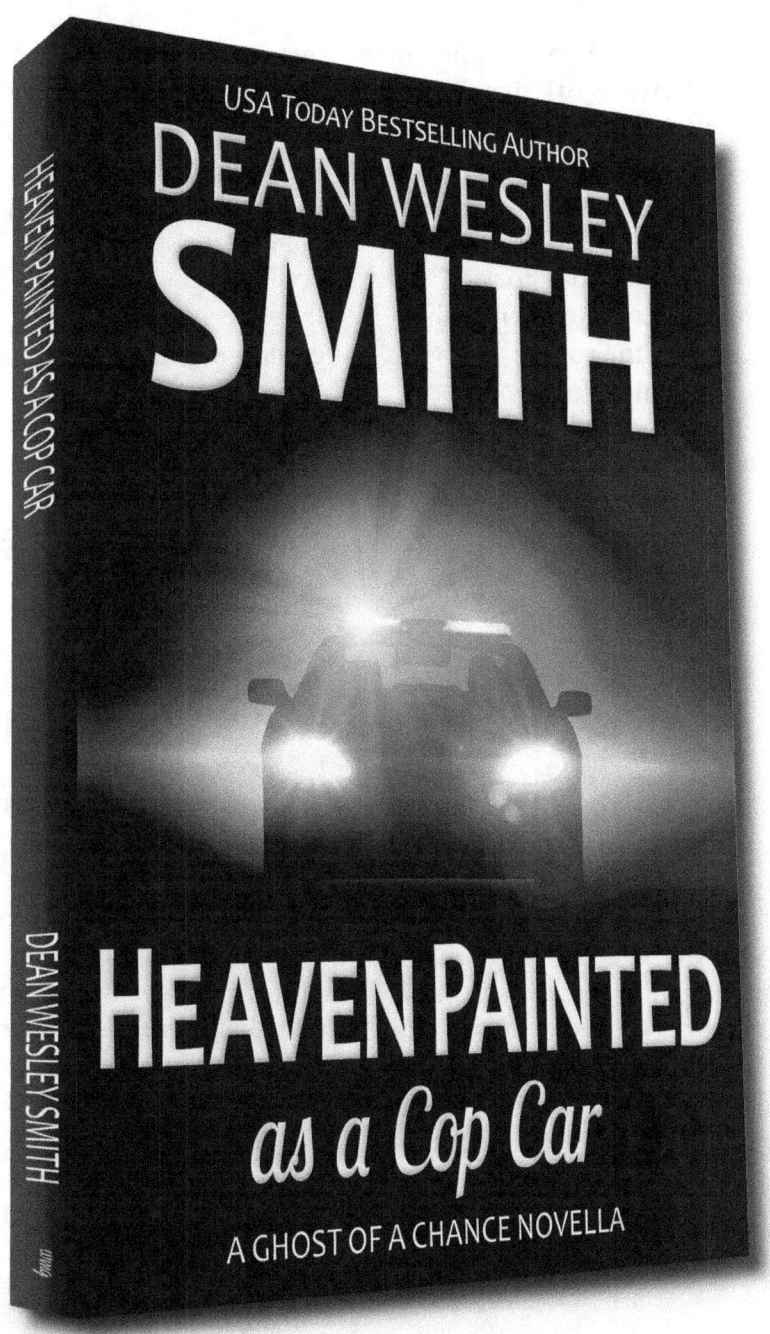

on the golf course. He couldn't believe what he had just heard. And he didn't want to think about what those words seemed to mean.

Bonnie finished putting on her shoes and he followed suit, not saying anything. He stood and made sure the men were long out of sight, then went out and grabbed his underwear off the fairway, stuffing them into his pocket as he turned.

He joined Bonnie on the cart path, headed back toward the clubhouse. After about ten steps he whispered, "Did that sound to you like it sounded to me?"

She put her finger up to his mouth and shook her head. "In the room," she whispered, just loud enough for him to hear.

Then she took his hand and they headed toward the beautiful hotel at a much faster pace than the stroll that got them there.

CHAPTER FOUR

Friday, April 7th
10:07 p.m.

THE WALK BACK to the hotel and up to their room seemed to take forever for Bonnie. Her heart was racing and her mind twisting at what they had overheard out on the course. She desperately wanted to talk to Craig about it, but knew that they didn't dare until they were safely in private. Just as they had discovered, voices carried on that golf course, especially at night.

After Craig closed the door behind them in their room, she dropped down onto the bed, enjoying the softness of

the mattress and the silky feel of the bedspread. "Tell me what you heard."

Craig paced between her and the dark television, a frown on his face. "Two men talking about causing a Senator to have an accident."

Bonnie nodded, her stomach now even more in a knot than it was on the walk back. "That's what I heard as well. Could we have misunderstood?"

"I've been wondering the exact same thing," Craig said, still pacing. "And the answer is yes, of course we could. They could have been talking about a game they were playing. Or the word accident could mean something completely different to them."

"Like what?" Bonnie asked, wanting to believe him, but not really following his logic.

Craig stopped and faced her. "They said they were going to do a Senator, right?"

Bonnie nodded. Those were the words she remembered very clearly.

"Who knows," Craig said, "maybe they were talking about getting a hooker for a senator and accident was how they were describing it."

Bonnie laughed, but she knew Craig was right. A single part of an overheard conversation could mean so many things, they didn't dare jump to too many conclusions. Especially the conclusions they were both jumping to.

"So what do we do now?" she asked.

"I suppose we should take things one step at a time," Craig said. He glanced at the clock on the stand beside the bed. "It's only a little after ten. Let's find out if there's a Senator registered here."

"And just how do you plan to do that?" she asked. "I doubt anyone is just going to tell you."

"You would be surprised," he said, smiling. He picked up the phone and punched a button.

Bonnie lay back on the bed. She could still feel the tingle from the fun they had had on the fairway. It had been intense, that much was for sure. And even more startling that they could fall asleep nude like that in the middle of a fairway afterwards. The thought made her smile.

If she had her way, there were going to a few more encounters just like that one before this weekend was over.

As soon as they got all this stuff settled.

"Front desk?" Craig asked. Then after a moment he said casually, as if he said the words every day, "Would you connect me to the Senator's head-of-staff, please?"

"Good thinking," she whispered, smiling at her husband. "but it won't work." Craig was such a good detective, she knew. And he had ways of getting information that most people would never think of. But a stranger didn't just go calling a hotel front desk and ask if a United States Senator was staying there. It didn't work that way. Important people had layers between themselves and the regular public. Protective and necessary layers because of all the nut cases in the world.

Of course, Craig hadn't asked to talk to a Senator, but instead he had asked for the Senator's head-of-staff. That detail might make all the difference.

"I'm being connected," he said, his eyes suddenly full of worry. He was clearly as surprised as she was, both at his idea working, and the fact that there was a Senator staying here.

"Oh, shit," she said, suddenly remembering why Craig was making the call.

"There is a Senator here. Now what are we going to do?"

He held his hand up. "Yes, hello, uh... Senator Knight," Craig said, giving her the wide-eyed shock look.

Craig was actually talking to Senator Knight! Bonnie thought her stomach was going to jump out of her body. Senator Knight from California was one of the more powerful Senators in all of Washington. What was he doing here? And what was he doing answering his own damned phone?

Craig went on, clearly deciding to tell the truth as he went. "My name is Detective Craig Frakes from Seattle. I'm sorry to bother you, but my wife and I overheard a conversation this evening that I think we should relay to you and your security staff, if you have a few moments."

Bonnie watched as Craig listened to the Senator. Then he said, "I don't honestly know how important it is, Senator. I suspect you would be the best one to judge that."

Craig nodded, then said, "Yes, sir. From Seattle. I can give you some names to call to check on who we are."

There was another long pause then Craig finished with, "Thank you, Senator, we'll be right up."

He hung up, then turned and smiled at her. "Better comb the grass out of your hair. We're about to meet Senator Knight."

"Wonderful," she said, shaking her head as she jumped to her feet and headed for the bathroom. "He's going to think we're a couple of nutballs, you know that, don't you?"

Craig laughed. "More than likely. But at least our consciences will be clear. He can decide to do what he wants with the information we heard."

He followed her into the bathroom as she grabbed a comb from their travel kit and started to brush the dried grass from her hair. She looked ruffled, and she doubted she was going to change that much in the few moments they had.

Craig reached under her arm and cupped her right breast, giving it a light squeeze. "Just checking to make sure they got put back into the right place."

She smiled at him. "Looks who's talking." She pointed at the lump in the front of his pants. "You might want to take your underwear out of your pocket. We don't want the Senator getting wrong ideas."

Craig laughed and pulled his underwear out and tossed them at the suitcase.

"We better take our badges with us," she said, putting the comb down and grabbing her purse, even though it didn't go with her shorts and blouse. "If I were the Senator's people, I'd damned well want to see them."

"Good thinking," Craig said, moving to dig his out of his suitcase. Bonnie knew that when traveling he never liked to carry it. He figured it would get him in more trouble than it was worth. But this time was different.

"And one more thing we might want to think about before we go up there," she said.

"And that is?" Craig asked as he stuffed his badge in his back pocket.

"What happens if one of the Senator's people is one of the people we overheard?"

"Shit," Craig said softly. He had clearly not thought about that possibility. "Would you recognize either voice?"

"Easily," she said. She doubted she would ever forget those two voices.

He nodded. "I think I would too. We're just going to have to chance it. And play it by ear if one of them is there."

She didn't much like playing a situation like this "by ear," but it seemed they had no choice.

Five minutes later they were on the top floor knocking on Senator Knight's door. Bonnie could feel the knot grow in her stomach as they waited. This was just plain crazy. How did they go from making love on a fairway to talking to a powerful United States Senator in the space of an hour? This was turning out to be one really strange vacation, and they hadn't even gotten through the first evening yet.

A young-looking man that Bonnie guessed to be no more than twenty-five, opened the door and nodded. "Identification please?"

Bonnie sighed at the sound of his voice. The young man clearly was not one of the men they had heard. She could tell Craig knew that as well.

Bonnie retrieved her badge from her purse while Craig showed his.

There was a moment of uneasy tension as the man studied both badges. "Seems fine," he said, nodding and handing the badges back. Then he extended his hand, smiling. "Steve Parsons, Senator Knight's assistant. Come on in."

Craig shook his hand, then Bonnie did. Parsons' hand felt firm and warm, and his smile was winning without being too patronizing. Bonnie liked this guy at first glance. More than likely it was that skill that had gotten him the job with a powerful senator at such a young age.

"Sorry to bother you and the Senator like this," Craig said as Parsons led them into the massive suite, "but we felt we had to tell someone what we heard."

"No problem," Parsons said. "We were just finishing up some paperwork before the weekend golf tournament. You can never get away from the stuff."

"I know how that feels," Craig said.

Bonnie got into the main area of the suite and simply stopped and stared. She had thought their room to be wonderful, but now it seemed much more like a regular hotel room. This suite clearly had numerous bedrooms and a massive living room and kitchen, all decorated in the soft earth and wood tones. The square footage was clearly more than their entire home.

"You sure got me intrigued," a voice came from around the corner in the kitchen. It also wasn't one of the voices on the path.

A moment later a refrigerator door closed and Senator Knight stepped toward them. He was holding a can of soda and wearing golf slacks and a polo shirt. He was also barefoot.

Bonnie was taken aback at the man's presence. His full head of gray hair seemed to shimmer and his smile filled the room. He extended his hand to her first. "I'm Darren Knight," he said, his voice firm.

Bonnie shook his firm hand and returned his smile. "Bonnie Stanley," she said. "And this is my husband, Craig Frakes."

"Pleased to meet you, Senator," Craig said.

"Likewise, Detective," the Senator said, indicating they should take a seat. "And just so you know, on your way up here Parsons there called Seattle to make sure you two are who you say you are. You got glowing recommendations all around."

"Nice to know," Bonnie said.

"So what's this all about?" the Senator asked as he dropped down into one of the big chairs. Parsons took the other, leaving the massive couch to Craig and Bonnie.

Bonnie sat back, leaving Craig to sit on the edge of the couch and do the talking.

Craig explained that he and Bonnie had gone out for a walk and decided to sit behind a rock near the cart path to watch the stars.

At that Senator Knight gave her a smile. Bonnie could feel her face redden slightly. She had no doubt the Senator knew what they had been doing, but had the good taste to say nothing.

"We heard two voices coming down the path from the hotel," Craig said. "Men's voices."

"And they were talking about me?" Senator Knight asked.

"I honestly don't know," Craig said. "Let me see if I can tell you word-for-word what we heard."

Bonnie listened as Craig went on to tell the Senator almost exactly the conversation they had heard. She doubted she could have relayed the words so accurately, but that was part of what Craig did every day.

When he had finished, Senator Knight turned to Bonnie. "Is this what you heard as well?" he asked. "Did your husband miss anything?"

She liked the man's question. He was being careful and making sure everything was clear. "I don't think he missed a word, Senator," Bonnie said. "And he added nothing."

The Senator nodded. "They didn't know you were there?"

"They didn't," Craig said. "And we made sure they were long gone before we moved. We went back to our room. We didn't know of any senator near here, so I called the desk, asking to be put through to someone on the Senator's staff, to see if there was even a senator here. They connected me to you."

"They did?" Parsons said, shaking his head. "That will change."

Bonnie smiled at the guy. Clearly someone in the hotel had screwed up and Parsons was going to make sure it didn't happen again.

Craig went on. "Can you see why we thought you and your security people should be notified?"

The Senator laughed. "Sure, but I'm afraid you are looking at my security team and my entire traveling staff."

Parsons sort of half-waved at Bonnie's stunned look.

Bonnie was shocked. She didn't know why, but she expected someone as important as Senator Knight to have security around him.

"Oh," Craig said, glancing at Parsons who only looked worried in return.

You know," the Senator said, laughing, "I get threats and hate mail all the time in my line of work. Almost all of them turn out to be nut cases. Harmless fools who think that threatening a Senator will get something done."

"Has anyone threatened you here?" Bonnie asked, not really believing that the Senator wasn't worried.

"Nope," the Senator said. "Just here to play a few days golf in this charity tournament on my way back to Washington."

"Senator," Craig said, "I also deal with nut cases every day. And I don't think this is one time that should be taken lightly."

"I agree," Parsons said.

The Senator looked at Bonnie.

She nodded. "This sounded very serious. And since it is not something you knew about, or two of your staff speaking in a code, we have to assume the two men's words meant what we thought."

"Is there any kind of government protection you could get?" Craig asked.

The Senator laughed, his smile filling the room. Bonnie had never seen someone so assured and comfortable in such an odd situation.

"I'm afraid there isn't much," the Senator said.

"And really nothing that could help us this weekend," Parsons said. "The Capital security is geared to function in Washington."

"How about the Secret Service?" Bonnie asked. "Or maybe the FBI?"

The Senator shook his head. "Mostly the Secret Service is only for the President and past Presidents, Vice Presidents, top White House Staff, Cabinet members, and others in direct line of succession to the Presidency. That bunch keeps them more than busy."

"We should call the local FBI," Parsons said, nodding to Bonnie.

She smiled back. She knew there had to be some branch of government who could help protect a Senator.

The Senator nodded and looked at Craig. "You don't mind telling the FBI what you heard?"

"Not at all," Craig said. "There's also an ex-Seattle cop working as a detective in the Scottsdale police force. I could give him a call as well."

Before the Senator could object, Parsons said, "I think that would be a good idea, Detective."

The Senator smiled at his assistant. "Just don't think of canceling me out of this golf tournament. I've been looking forward to this for a month."

"So have we," Bonnie said. And if she had her way, this problem wasn't going to get in the way of either the golf tournament or their vacation.

CHAPTER FIVE

Friday, April 7th
10:39 p.m.

THE HEAT HAD been almost too much for Steph Baines to bear. The men with weapons had led her out of her apartment and into the back of an older panel van. The windows in the back doors had been covered and there was a partition between the cargo area and the front seats that had no door or window in it.

When the van's doors were closed, two of the masked men had tied her up and put her on the metal floor in the back of the van. Her feet were tied with a twine that cut into the flesh around her ankles and her hands were yanked behind her back and tied with a softer rope.

Then they had left, shutting and clearly latching the van door. Then she had heard them climb into the front of the van and start the engine. She could sit up, but not comfortably. Every corner the van took had sent her sprawling on the metal floor. Finally, after twenty minutes of trying to stay sitting, she had given up and remained on her side, her feet braced against the side of the van to help stop her from sliding around.

This was all the worst nightmare she could have ever imagined. She had simply taken the morning off from school to help Danny get ready for the weekend golf tournament. During the entire drive all she could think was wonder why had they picked her?

And what did they have in mind for her?

She had tried not to think about that second question, mostly without luck.

Everything her imagination had come up with was too horrible to even consider.

For an eternity the van had seemed to drive on a freeway. She had moved around enough to find a half-comfortable position. The heat also kept getting worse and worse and sweat ended up coating her skin and streaking her with the dirt and dust from the floor.

During one smooth stretch of road she had managed to move over to a sharp edge sticking out of one wall and work the rope around her wrists against it. But before she could get it cut, the van had jerked and she had cut herself. Her blood had felt warm dripping off her fingers and down her back. She had had no idea how bad she had sliced herself, but she hadn't tried cutting the rope again. After a few minutes the bleeding had stopped. She had no doubt that if she had cut herself deeply, she would have bled to death before any of the men even noticed or cared.

Finally, after a bunch of turns and starts and stops, the van had stopped and the engine had shut off.

No one had opened the door to the van.

No one had come to give her water.

The sun had just baked the van into an oven.

For an eternity she had just sat there until finally she lay down and let the heat take her.

The next thing she knew a man was saying, "Here, drink this."

She felt wonderful, cool water pour over her lips and she had managed to choke a little of it down.

"Stupid idiots," the man said. "They almost killed you."

She had let more of the water in and swallowed, then had opened her eyes enough to see the unmasked man who had kidnapped her.

The guy smiled. "Good, glad you're still with us lady." He turned to someone beside her that she couldn't see. "Take her inside and get her situated in the second bathroom."

She had felt hands roughly pick her up and carry her just before the world left her again.

Now the darkness seemed to push back one more time as she came to again. This time she was lying on a soft rug on a small bathroom floor. Her hands and feet were untied and a bright light was on over the bathroom mirror.

Slowly, fighting the dizziness, she pulled herself up to a kneeling position and turned on the water in the sink. Using her hand as a cup she managed to drink a little more before slumping back to the wonderful coolness of the floor.

She just knew that in a short time she'd wake up beside Danny and this would all be a nightmare, that he would hold her and help her get over.

All she had to do was wake up.

She lay on her back, staring up at the bathroom light, waiting.

But the nightmare just wouldn't go away.

CHAPTER SIX

Friday, April 7th
11:12 p.m.

IT HAD TAKEN Parsons two phone calls to get an FBI agent on the way.

Craig had used a second line at the same time to get in touch with Detective

Hagar Daniels, formally of Seattle, now part of the Scottsdale police force.

Twenty minutes later Hagar had arrived at the Senator's suite, followed in less than a minute by John Maxwell of the FBI.

Bonnie remembered Hagar from his time in the Seattle force. He was a big man, well over six-four, with broad shoulders, a small gut, and a sense of humor that seemed almost too dry. He arrived wearing white Bermuda shorts, a golf shirt, and sandals.

Maxwell, from the FBI, was even more casually dressed in jeans, a Grateful Dead tee-shirt, and a Phoenix Suns baseball cap. He stood about Craig's height at six foot, and was trim and clearly in shape. His most striking feature were his deep blue eyes that Bonnie felt saw everything.

Maxwell and Hagar clearly knew each other, and liked each other. Bonnie had a sneaking hunch they had worked together a number of times before and didn't have the rivalry that sometimes happened between local cops and the FBI.

After all the introductions and badge exchanges were finished, the Senator had the two new arrivals join them in the large living room area of the suite and then had Craig relay exactly, word-for-word, what he and Bonnie had heard.

Bonnie was again amazed at how exact he got everything. There were times her husband impressed her and this was one of them.

After Craig had finished with the story and how he had informed the Senator, Hagar whistled softly. Then he said, "No wonder you called us."

Maxwell faced the Senator. "You don't have any friends or co-workers here with you besides Mr. Parsons?"

Bonnie liked the question. It was along the same lines that she and Craig had first thought might be a possibility.

"I sure don't," Senator Knight said. "It's just the two of us. I seldom travel with anyone else, do I?"

Parsons nodded his agreement, but said nothing.

"No meetings planned this weekend?" Maxwell asked.

"Just with my putter and thirty-six holes of golf," the Senator said, laughing.

"One more question," Maxwell said. "Has any person in this area threatened you lately?"

The Senator looked at his assistant. "I never read those kind of letters," he said. "You know of anyone?"

Parsons shook his head slowly. "All the threatening letters are back in the office in Washington. I don't remember any lately from this area, but I could have that checked in the morning."

"I think getting someone to do it tonight might be a better idea," Craig said.

Bonnie completely agreed. The morning might be too late.

Maxwell nodded. "I agree. I'll have someone from the Washington bureau meet one of your staff members tonight to go through the letters."

Parsons laughed. "Jenny, the Senator's secretary, isn't going to be happy."

The Senator joined in. "Got that right. Monday in the office is going to be hell."

"Better than no Monday," Maxwell said seriously.

Bonnie agreed, but the Senator just waved a hand dismissing the somber tone. It seemed that even though this was his life they were all worried about, the Senator wasn't going to let it bother him. He was here to have fun and damned if he was going to let anything like someone threatening his life get in the way.

But if he wasn't going to be worried, Bonnie knew that the rest of them had to worry for him. Which meant they had to stay close to him, and during a golf tournament, that wasn't going to be easy to do.

"Senator?" Bonnie said, "who are you planning on playing with in the tournament tomorrow?"

"They got me scheduled with a young, hot pro from the Sedona area," the Senator said. "Beyond that, I don't have any idea."

"Well," Bonnie said, smiling at the Senator, "Craig and I are here to play as well. Mind if we join you?"

"Dear Ms. Stanley," the Senator said, "that would be my pleasure."

Bonnie could feel herself blushing slightly again. Why the Senator did that to her she had no idea. Out of the corner of her eye she could see both Craig and Hagar nodding, clearly agreeing with the idea of she and Craig playing the round with the Senator.

"Well, people," the Senator said, standing. "My tee time is at eight-forty-six in the morning, and I plan on getting a good night's sleep. Thank you all for your concern."

With that he headed into the bedroom to the right of the living area and shut the door.

His exit felt sudden to Bonnie, but correct. There was nothing more he could do now, so he left the planning in the hands of the people who knew what they were doing. He was clearly a person who knew how to delegate and was used to doing just that.

One hour later, Craig and Bonnie left, heading for their room.

Bonnie was tired, and they had to be up early for the tee time, but she knew

there was no chance she could get to sleep at once after all that had happened. She wasn't sure she was going to get much sleep the entire night.

An FBI agent was standing at the end of the corridor as they headed for the elevator, clearly on post for the evening. He nodded good night to them. Maxwell was efficient and already covering the Senator. That made Bonnie feel a lot better.

Bonnie had been impressed with both Maxwell and Hagar. After the Senator went to bed, the four of them had planned what measures were needed to guard someone on a rocky, desert golf course. Much of the close-in duty was going to fall on Bonnie and Craig's shoulders, and Hagar was going to furnish them both with side-arms tomorrow to carry in their golf bags just in case. Maxwell would ride in a cart along with the group as well, with his people and Hagar's people set up along the course in an unobtrusive manner.

Everything was being done that the four of them could think to do. Even Parsons seemed satisfied with the plans after getting off the phone with the Senator's staff in Washington.

The only thing they couldn't figure out was who would want the Senator hurt, and who would pay big money, as the two men on the path had said, to have it done? Both Hagar and Maxwell said they would have full teams working that end of the problem.

Bonnie and Craig rode in silence down the elevator and to their room.

As Craig opened the door she said, "Seems we're not going to get away from work after all."

"Yeah, I'm afraid we were in the wrong place at the wrong time."

Bonnie moved inside and Craig let the door close behind them, locking the safely bolt. Then he turned and she put her arms around his neck, kissing him lightly. "I thought it was fun out there on that fairway. Didn't you?"

Craig pulled her close and kissed her hard. Then he pulled back and smiled. "Lots of fun."

"Worth all these problems?"

He pretended to be serious. "Sex with you is never a problem and always worth it."

"Ahh, the right thing for a husband to say," she said, kissing him again. "The exact right thing."

CHAPTER SEVEN

Saturday, April 8th
8:04 a.m.

AT SLIGHTLY AFTER eight in the morning, the desert sun was still a good hour from completely taking the chill off the morning air. Craig hadn't bothered to grab a jacket when he left the room for breakfast, but after walking from the clubhouse to the cart area, he wished he had. He was only wearing golf slacks and a short-sleeved shirt. He knew that by noon he was going to be too warm, but right now he was darned cold.

No doubt Bonnie was as well. She had on a pair of tight white shorts and a thin, see-through blouse with a white halter-top underneath. It was an outfit that was sure to drive the Senator to distraction by the time the round was over. Watching that wonderful body in those tight shorts wasn't going to exactly help keep Craig's mind on the game either.

Right now, because of the cold, Bonnie's nipples were clearly visible as sharp bumps standing out against the halter-top and blouse. She had her arms crossed under her breasts for warmth, not covering anything.

About a hundred identical golf carts were all lined two abreast along a wide area of concrete to one side of the clubhouse, ready to go for the tournament. Each pair of carts had white pieces of paper with different tee-times on the steering wheels.

Craig and Bonnie moved down the line until they found their 8:46 time that Hagar had arranged last night with the tournament staff. Their golf clubs were already loaded into two carts, Bonnie's in the cart with Senator Knight's bag and Craig's beside a large black bag that had the word Titleist covering one side. Clearly Craig was riding with the pro and Bonnie was riding with the Senator.

Craig wasn't too sure if he liked the idea of Bonnie being that close to the possible target of an assassin, but he couldn't think of any logical reason to change the pairing.

There were a lot of people coming and going from around the carts and bags, but there was no sign of the Senator or Maxwell or Hagar.

"Damn, it's cold out here," Bonnie said, grabbing her visor from the front pocket of her bag.

"Wait an hour and that will change," Craig said.

"I may be frozen stiff in an hour," Bonnie said.

"Parts of you already are stiff," Craig said, glancing down at where her nipples were trying to break free from her blouse.

She smacked his arm in mock anger, but he could tell she was enjoying the attention.

"Excuse me, Detective Craig and Officer Stanley," a man said, moving up beside them.

Craig glanced up as a guy in blue slacks and white jacket approached. He was either FBI, one of Hagar's men, or one of the golf pros. Craig would bet a month's salary on FBI.

"I'm Agent Howard," the man said. "The Senator is on the driving range. He told me to tell you to bring both the carts."

"Thanks," Craig said.

"One more thing," Agent Howard said, moving in so his voice could only be heard by Craig and Bonnie. "In the outside pocket of both your bags are loaded weapons. Detective Hagar wanted me to make sure you knew where they were."

Craig nodded and turned to his bag. He unzipped the outside pocket just enough to see the handle of the police special stuffed down in his rain gear. It was the exact same model as his gun back in Seattle.

"Got it," he said, zipping up the pocket and turning back to the agent.

Bonnie looked up from her bag, a grim look on her face. "Should work fine if I have to use it."

"Let's hope we don't," Agent Howard said.

"Couldn't agree more," Craig said. "Thanks."

Agent Howard turned and moved away from them, walking down the row of carts as if he belonged here.

"I wonder how many other FBI and Scottsdale police are around," Bonnie said.

"More than we're going to spot," Craig said, "if they are doing their job."

Craig moved over and sat down on the cold cart seat. "Follow me."

Bonnie dropped down behind the wheel of the other cart, then said, "Holy shit, that's cold."

Craig laughed.

"What's so funny?" Bonnie asked, glaring at him. "I didn't come to Arizona to freeze my ass off."

"Trust me," Craig said, turning the cart out of line and starting toward the driving range. "You'll be wishing for a cold seat in two hours."

He couldn't hear Bonnie's answer.

The path to the driving range was at least four hundred yards of winding pavement that led up over the top of a rock bluff and down into a steep valley hidden from the clubhouse. The wind in his face was biting-cold, and he drove with only one hand, keeping the other under his leg for some warmth.

As he cleared the top of the ridge, he was colder than he could remember being in a long, long time.

The driving range spread out below him, filling a massive open area of green that sloped down the floor of the rock-sided valley. Colored flags were placed at different distances from the teeing area.

Twenty or so people were scattered over the teeing area that looked like it could hold at least fifty people hitting balls at the same time. Each player had his or her own area marked by a metal stand to lean clubs against, a small rock, and a shining pile of red-striped golf balls. Craig loved the free driving-range balls when coming to the desert. Back in the Northwest, driving-range balls were normally sold by the bucket. Down here they just piled them up for every player to use as many as they wanted.

Maxwell was sitting in a cart just off the path on the far side of the range and

Hagar and two others were talking off to the right side.

Craig waved at them and then looked around for the Senator. He was at the far left side of the range, his back to the hill and Maxwell. It was the easiest spot to guard in the entire area.

Craig took the cart down the path, parking it directly behind the Senator. Bonnie pulled up behind him, clearly even colder than she had been back at the clubhouse. Her fingers looked white as she blew on them, and Craig could swear her teeth were chattering.

"Are we having fun yet?" he asked, smiling at her.

She only glared at him and moved around to get some clubs out of her bag.

"Not yet, huh?" he said, laughing as he grabbed a few clubs and headed to a pile of balls. The Senator glanced up and said, "Good morning."

"Morning, sir," Craig said.

The Senator was wearing green Bermuda shorts and a Hawaiian shirt that would clash with anything. He had on white socks and black golf shoes. Anyone trying to take a shot at this guy would be laughing too hard to shoot straight.

"Good morning, Senator," Bonnie said, walking up and standing behind him. "You look colorful this morning."

The Senator laughed. "A natural politician. I knew I liked you for more than your fantastic looks."

Bonnie blushed. Craig could very seldom get that kind of reaction out of her, yet the Senator seemed to be able to do it at will.

The Senator pointed to a man two spots over hitting balls with a fluid golf swing. "Craig, Bonnie, that is Danny Baines. From Sedona."

Danny turned and stepped toward them, his hand outstretched, a smile filling his face. Danny had to be all of twenty, if that. He had the kind of face that Craig figured women loved. Sort of a cross between Paul McCartney and Paul Newman. But there was something about him that bothered Craig almost instantly. And he wasn't sure what it was.

"Nice to meet you both," the kid-pro said. "Looking forward to our round."

"Yeah," Bonnie said. "Me too."

After she had shaken the kid's hand, she turned and gave Craig the eyebrows-up, wide-eyed look. He wasn't sure if that meant she thought the kid was hot, or if it meant she was feeling the same way he was. He'd ask her when he got a chance.

Thirty minutes later, Craig rolled his drive off the first tee, the Senator hit his drive into a large pile of rocks to the left of the fairway, and Bonnie and the pro hit the fairway. It was a good indication of how the day would go.

CHAPTER EIGHT

Saturday, April 8th
12:44 p.m.

BONNIE FIGURED SHE had gotten the best deal, riding with the Senator. He was charming, laughed easily, and was determined to have fun, no matter how bad his golf game was. And it was bad, plain and simple.

The first hole he had managed a nine from the rocks, and except for a bogey four on a short par three, that was his best score. The good thing was that he didn't take much time over any single shot. He just walked up to it, took his stance and hit it, often sideways and never very far.

The young pro was another matter. He was the silent type who had had it two under par by the end of the first nine, and took lots of time over each shot. However, he had taken so many fewer shots than the rest of them, it didn't really slow them down at all.

Also the kid hadn't said much more than "Nice shot!" or "Your turn," the entire morning. Bonnie hadn't been able to figure out what bothered her about the kid, but one thing for sure, he had a beautiful golf swing.

The Senator had Bonnie so relaxed with his jokes and friendly patter that by the second hole, even with the distraction of always looking around, always being aware of any danger, she had played well.

Far better than Craig had, that was for sure.

The temperature had finally warmed up enough to be comfortable by the third hole, and by the time they had reached the tenth hole it was warm. By the scenic sixteenth hole tee box on the back nine, it was just plain hot.

The sixteenth was a fairly long par three, with the tee boxes for the hole carved out of the side of a large hill, and the green a good hundred feet below them across a deep rock canyon. The group in front of them was still on the green, so Bonnie climbed up the dirt and wood steps to get on the highest tee box. Maxwell and another FBI agent were already up there, off to one side, scanning the surrounding area.

The light wind blew at her blouse and hair, cooling her as she looked around. The view was just spectacular. Where she stood was by far the highest place on the golf course, and from there she could see out over Scottsdale and Phoenix.

"Wow," Senator Knight said, moving up to stand beside her. "This is a sight."

"I didn't know Senators were prone to understatement," Bonnie said.

The Senator laughed. "The spectacular view took my words away."

"That's better," Bonnie said, smiling at him.

Below them the cart path wound back and forth, switchback after switchback, down the almost cliff-steep side of the mountain between the tee box and the green.

And there were dirt footpaths in the rocks and scrub brush leading down into the canyon where golfers had climbed down to search for balls. If she hit one down in there, she wasn't going down looking for it, that was for sure. Too many snake-warning signs around this course for her tastes. Since she saw the first sign back on the fifth hole, she hadn't gotten off the cart path or fairway without a club in her hand.

Two of Hagar's men stood on the hill on the far side of the hole, waiting. She could imagine how boring the day had been for them. Climbing around in the rocks and desert, watching four people play golf.

Thank heavens that was all that had happened so far.

Craig moved up beside her and whispered in her ear. "What do you say we come back up here tonight?"

"And do what?" she whispered back, teasing him.

"An encore performance," he said, just loud enough for her to hear.

"Sex on the top of a mountain," she whispered. "I like that idea. As long as you carry me up here."

Craig laughed and said loud enough for the Senator to hear. "It might just be worth it."

The Senator gave her a raised-eyebrow look and Bonnie could feel herself blush again.

Then he said, smiling at her, "Green's open."

What seemed like an outrageous distance below her the foursome in front of them cleared the green and Danny moved to the tee.

His shot sailed into the air and then seemed to drop forever. At first she thought it was going to be so far over the green that it might land on one of Hagar's men on the far hillside. But finally the ball dropped about twenty paces short of the pin, bounced once and stopped. In all the years she had played golf, she had never been on a hole like this.

She hit two balls into the canyon before she declared she was done and was going to drop a ball up by the green. This might be the most spectacular vista in the desert, but it was also one impossible golf hole.

Craig managed to hit one over the canyon, landing it on the right of the green and they all cheered him like he'd just hit a home run. As far as Bonnie was concerned, that was his best shot of the day.

Even Maxwell applauded.

The Senator rolled a shot off the end of the tee box. They all watched as the ball bounced, clattered, and fell like a pinball gone crazy down the rocky slope. It bounced twice on the cart path, once about twenty feet below the tee box, and a second time somewhere even with the green about three switchbacks down. The ball finally disappeared into the canyon in front of the green.

The Senator glanced over at Danny.

"I think that ball went four hundred yards at least, if you count every bounce."

Danny nodded. "Thank your lucky stars it didn't get stuck somewhere on that cliff. You would have had to try to hit it."

"Not in this lifetime," the Senator said, glancing down the steep, rocky slope.

The Senator tried one more shot—this time flying his ball into the canyon—and decided Bonnie's idea of dropping one on the other side was the best policy. Everyone agreed.

Bonnie climbed into the cart beside the Senator and stared at the sign twenty feet in front of them.

WARNING!
STEEP DOWNGRADE.
SLOW!
USE BRAKES!

Thank heavens the Senator took the warning to heart. The hole was no more than one hundred and seventy yards as the crow flies, but the cart path down that cliff face had to be five times that long. And very, very narrow and steep. She was sweating more from the fear than the heat by the time they reached the flat bridge over the canyon in front of the green.

The Senator's knuckles were white on the steering wheel.

It was a golf hole, and a golf cart ride she would never forget.

They made it the rest of the way through the round without problems, and the Senator agreed to meet them in the bar for drinks after a shower and change of clothes.

"You don't mind, do you Senator," Craig asked, "if we play with you again tomorrow?"

Hagar and Maxwell were both standing close by and both nodded their agreement with the idea.

"Sounds fine with me," the Senator said. "As long as Bonnie wears those white shorts again."

For the fifth or sixth time, Bonnie blushed. Why he could do that to her, she didn't know.

"She has another pair that is even tighter," Craig said, winking at the Senator.

Bonnie punched him in the arm as the Senator laughed. She did have a tighter pair, and now she planned on wearing them for sure.

"Then I look forward to the round," the Senator said. "I'll meet you in the bar in an hour."

Bonnie glanced at her watch. It was a little after two in the afternoon. A shower sounded perfect to help cool down and rinse off a layer of suntan lotion.

"Sounds great," Craig said.

"Drinks and dinner are on me," the Senator said. "For all of you. No arguments." He glanced at Maxwell and Hagar, who both nodded, then at Bonnie.

"It sounds like a wonderful time," she said.

"Good. An hour then." He turned and headed up into the hotel.

Maxwell moved with him and Bonnie had no doubt there were other FBI agents working ahead of the Senator. She really liked the guy, even though he made her blush with the slightest look. She was glad they were doing everything in their power to make sure nothing happened to him.

So far all was well. But there was still the rest of the afternoon and tonight.

And all of tomorrow.

CHAPTER NINE

Saturday, April 8th
9:07 p.m.

AFTER A QUICK shower in the strange waterfall tub, Craig had ended up having two rum and cokes in the bar. Those drinks, combined with a lot of laugher and jokes, had stretched over two hours. It had been almost six by the time they finally went into the restaurant for dinner, and Craig had been famished.

Bonnie had only had one drink and a lot of water and she whispered to him as they walked into the restaurant that she was so hungry, she was about to eat the bar napkins.

Parsons, Hagar and Maxwell had joined them in the bar. Parsons said he didn't drink and Hagar and Maxwell had both stuck to Diet Cokes since they were on duty. Craig could see a few other detectives and agents stationed around the bar and restaurant.

The food had turned out to be even better than Craig would have expected, and his expectations were high in this beautiful resort. He had had a perfectly cooked New York steak, while Bonnie had lamb.

The food was so good, Craig just didn't want to stop eating.

Finally, at nine the Senator excused himself, saying it was time to get back to his room, do a little work, and get some sleep, since their tee time in the morning was 8:15.

Maxwell and Hagar left the table with the Senator and Parsons, leaving only Craig and Bonnie. As she pushed away the last few bites of her raspberry-covered cheesecake she moaned.

"Full?"

"Stuffed like a turkey at Thanksgiving," she said, sipping on her coffee.

"Before or after roasting?"

She touched her suntanned arm. "After, clearly."

"So what do you say we go for a walk?" Craig asked. "It's getting dark."

"To walk off the dinner, or did you have something else in mind?'

"Maybe both," he said.

"Perfect."

Hand in hand they strolled out of the restaurant and through the lobby. Not only was the restaurant and bar still busy, but so was the central area of the massive hotel. Craig figured at least a hundred people milled around in the vast wood and stone space, talking and laughing and generally enjoying the party atmosphere of the charity golf tournament. Even with the fear for the Senator, he was enjoying himself as well.

And, it seemed, Bonnie was too.

"Let's go out this way," Craig said, pulling Bonnie through the lobby away from the front door and down a wide hallway that led to the pro shop area. He knew there was another door there that went out toward the back nine.

Last night they had gone out the front and ended up on the second hole. When they went past the spot this morning Bonnie had pointed out to the Senator where they were sitting when they overheard the men. The Senator's only comment was, "It looks like a nice private spot to me."

Bonnie had blushed.

Craig was enjoying the fact that the Senator could make her blush with a simple comment.

The Pro Shop was closed, so Craig led Bonnie down the wide staircase to an outside door between the entrances to the locker rooms. Where the carts had been lined up early that morning was an empty expanse of concrete. To the left Craig could see a large, open door behind a massive boulder. It looked as if it led down into what was clearly a cart storage area under the hotel.

There was no one around. Compared to the massive number of people just a short distance away in the lobby and restaurant area, it felt odd to be alone.

Bonnie ambled toward the open door. "I wonder how many carts a place like this has?"

"They have two courses here," he said. "It has to be a lot. A couple hundred at least." He followed her down the ramp around the rock and into a massive, low-ceilinged garage area.

"Try four or five hundred," Bonnie said.

Craig stood in the door beside her, amazed at the expanse of lined up carts that seemed to almost vanish into the distance in the dim light. They were in perfect rows, with cords draping from the ceiling. Each cord was plugged into a cart in the center under the seat.

To Craig it looked like each was hooked into an umbilical cord.

The carts were all empty and cleaned, waiting, the clubs clearly off in a locked storage area somewhere.

Bonnie walked slowly down one aisle. Each cart was numbered, and that number matched a number painted on the concrete. It looked like something he'd seen in a bad science fiction movie: aliens waiting to be activated. And the dim light didn't help the image.

"I wonder what their power bill is like for all this," Bonnie said, pointing up at all the chargers on shelves along one ceiling beam.

Craig followed, not sure that they should be in there, but not stopping either.

Bonnie glanced over at Craig. "You remember what our cart numbers were today?"

"You and the Senator had 167 and Danny and I had 168," he said, surprised at himself for remembering. But since he and Danny had been following the Senator's cart all day, and the number to their cart was on the back right bumper, it had pretty much stuck in his mind.

They were walking along the carts with low eighties for numbers. Bonnie kept going, deeper into the dimly-lit room. He had no idea what she had in mind, but he followed anyway.

She led him between cart 104 and 105 over to the next row. Cart 167 was backed against the concrete wall five or six carts from the back of the room. Bonnie climbed in and patted the seat beside her.

"Just what are we doing?" Craig asked, sliding into the passenger seat.

"Shhh," she said softly. "Just listen."

The silence seemed to suddenly get louder than his own heartbeat as they sat there in the darkness. The light from the door they had come in was the only bright area. The rest of the massive garage was illuminated by dim nightlights scattered on support pillars. There was a faint hum that filled the air, more than likely coming from the chargers above each cart.

Nothing else.

Bonnie moved her hand to his lap and squeezed. Then she whispered, "Every time you climbed in the cart today I wanted to do that."

"Don't stop now," he whispered back.

Her hand worked over his crotch, rubbing him through his slacks, making him grow quickly hard.

"Nice," he whispered. "Very nice." He leaned into her and they kissed, long and hard, the taste of the cheesecake dessert covering her breath like a sweet mint.

He moved his hands up to her breasts, rubbing them through her blouse and bra. He felt like a high school kid again, out parking on a date, touching a girl's breasts through her blouse. Those nights were exciting and frustrating at the same time. He had loved the feeling and had always wished he could recapture it.

Now he was and it was great.

Excitement of being in a different place combined with sexual touching, all wrapped into the fear of getting caught. This weekend was going to be memorable for a number of things.

Bonnie seemed to be enjoying it just like his dates had back then. Actually, he was enjoying it more than he had in high school, since none of his dates had ever put her hand on his crotch like Bonnie was doing now.

They kissed again, long and hard and passionately. It seemed it had been years since the two of them had felt so passionate with each other. Craig knew right then they were going to have to take vacations much more often.

Bonnie started fumbling to unzip his pants and open his belt. He broke the kiss to help, but before he could get his belt undone the sound of something metal dropping echoed through the massive empty room.

Both Bonnie and Craig jerked away from each other to stare out through the carts. Craig thought his heart was going to jump right out of his chest from the shock. Across the massive garage, at least six rows over, Craig could see two men moving toward the door.

He couldn't see their faces, since their backs were mostly turned toward them, but one had short hair, the other wore a golf cap. Both looked to be about six foot, one had wider shoulders than the other.

As the two neared the door, one spoke, clearly loud enough for Bonnie and Craig to hear. "Man, you two need to get a room."

Then the two men were gone out the door and up the ramp.

Craig glanced at the shocked look on Bonnie's face. Instantly he knew she thought the same thing he did. That voice was one of the voices from last night.

"Come on," he said, jumping out of the cart and running down the aisle toward the door, making sure his zipper was up as he ran.

"We don't have our guns," Bonnie said from behind him.

Craig knew that. "I don't plan on stopping them. Just following."

At the large door he stopped and quickly peered around the corner. As he had expected, they were not in sight up the ramp. With Bonnie right behind him he ran up to the door into the clubhouse. There were two couples walking out near one of the putting greens, and a maintenance man working in the ground near a planter, but no sign of the two men.

"They must have gone inside," Bonnie said, pointing to the double doors that led past the pro shop and up the stairs.

Craig agreed. It was the only place they could have gone that quickly.

At a run they went back up the stairs, down the hall, and into the main lobby. There seemed to be even more people up here than there had when they left a half hour before.

He and Bonnie moved to one side and stood, scanning the people. Not a sign of the two men.

They had vanished.

"Damn," Bonnie said.

Craig couldn't agree more. "We need to inform Maxwell and Hagar. Let's head up to the Senator's floor."

"Just don't tell the Senator what we were doing," Bonnie said. "I get embarrassed enough around that man."

"Agreed," Craig said, smiling. "But we have to tell the others what the guy said."

"Damn, damn, damn," Bonnie said. "Caught parking in a golf cart inside a garage. How bad is that?"

"And with a married man as well," Craig said. "What's your husband going to say?"

"I hope he says rain check."

"Rain check."

Ten minutes later, with Hagar and Maxwell and two other FBI agents with them, they did a sweep through the hotel lobby, bar, and restaurant, looking for two men who matched the vague description of what Bonnie and Craig had seen. No luck at all, which just made Craig even that much more frustrated.

They all then went back down to the cart storage area. With Bonnie's help, they managed to figure out which row the two men had seemed to suddenly appear in. Hagar got one of the hotel security staff to turn up the lights and they searched the entire area without finding anything.

Maxwell pointed at a regular-sized door in the back wall near the end of the cart aisle they were searching. "Maybe they came out of there." Maxwell glanced at one of the hotel security guards. "Where's that lead?"

"Service area," the security guard said.

"We didn't hear a door open or close," Craig said. He glanced at Bonnie to make sure and she nodded her agreement.

"They might have already come through it when we came in," Bonnie said.

Maxwell nodded and moved to the door. It was locked, but the security guard quickly had it open. The door was the kind that could be opened from the inside even if locked so the two men could have easily come through it from the inside. Behind the door was a staircase leading upwards into a main floor service area of the hotel. And right across from where the staircase came out were three service elevators.

"It seems the two we are looking for know their way around this place," Bonnie said.

"I hope you have those guarded," Craig said, pointing at the service elevators.

"On the Senator's floor we do," Maxwell said. "But I'm beginning to think we may need to cover the floor below as well."

Craig could only agree.

CHAPTER TEN

Saturday, April 8th
10:19 p.m.

CHARLES ROBINS MOVED out onto his patio toward the man standing there. Never had the man returned in the middle of an assignment before. And never had the man called him on his personal, unlisted number to set up a meeting so late.

Charles had paced for the last two hours, waiting, coming up with a dozen things that could have gone wrong. Clearly the Senator had not met with his accident yet, so something had. The question was what?

And how serious was the problem?

Finally the man in the dark suit had appeared on the patio, smoking as always.

"So what has gone wrong?" Charles demanded.

"You tell me," the man said, his voice low and very mean. "The Senator has clearly been tipped that something might happen to him this weekend. Both the Scottsdale authorities and the FBI are staying very close to him. And he is playing with two cops from Seattle."

Charles felt as if someone had punched him in the stomach. "How? I said nothing to anyone but you."

"Are you sure?" the man asked, his voice seemingly on the edge of anger, barely controlled. His eyes were like two black holes in the darkness, unblinking and deadly.

"Of course I'm sure," Charles said, disgusted. "If Senator Knight makes that vote on Monday, I'm as good as broke and in prison. It would only be a matter of time. So why the hell would I tell anyone I'm trying to stop him?"

"Well, they have discovered the threat to the Senator in some fashion," the man said.

"But can you still do what needs to be done?"

The man nodded. "The Senator can still meet his date with an accident. But it will cost you a great deal more than before. And this will be our last meeting ever."

"How much more?" Charles demanded. The man's fee hadn't been small before this setback.

The man laughed. "This is not a negotiation." He handed Charles a slip of paper.

Charles did not even give the man the satisfaction of looking down at the note.

"If the first amount specified is not in that off-shore numbered account by ten in the morning, the Senator will make his plane to Washington just fine."

"And if I put the money in the account and you do not carry through on your end of the deal?" Charles demanded, getting angrier and angrier.

"Then you do not have to pay the second, larger payment specified."

That made Charles glance down at the paper, but he could not read it in the dim light.

"And trust me," the man said, "if I carry through with my end of this and you do not pay the second amount, you will meet an accident far worse than what waits for the Senator. And far more painful."

"You are threatening me?" Charles demanded, stepping toward the man. Charles could not remember ever being so angry as to want to hit someone. But right now he was.

The man stood his ground, his dark eyes intense, his posture relaxed. "Of course I am."

Charles just stared at the man. This man was blackmailing him and there was nothing at all he could do about it. Charles was going to lose everything and the man knew it and was using that fact to extract everything he could.

"Think it over," the man said.

"How do I know you didn't make up this entire story about the FBI knowing there is a threat to the Senator?"

"You don't," the man said. "But it is the truth and there is no way to prove it to you."

Charles stared at the man. More than likely this guy had just been waiting for the right assignment from Charles to pull this blackmail stunt and then vanish. More than likely the man had done the same to other clients in the past and gotten away with it.

Well, he was going to get away with it again. Charles was desperate. Senator Knight had to be kept from that vote on Monday. There was no other choice.

"All right," Charles said. "The money will be in the account in the morning."

"It has been nice doing business with you," the man said, turning from Charles and starting across the patio.

"Just make sure it's done," Charles said.

"Oh, I will be successful," the man said without looking back. "You just make sure the payments are made and we can both live happily ever after."

With that the man walked down the path away from the patio and vanished into the night.

Charles turned and moved back into the light so that he could read the amounts on the paper. His stomach clamped up like the guy had punched him. $250,000 by ten in the morning. $750,000 within twelve hours of completion.

"Damn, damn, damn," he said, glancing around to see if the man was still in sight. That was a vast amount of money, yet possible. And the man he called Bill knew it. Its removal from his corporate accounts was going to be hard to hide, but better taking a chance with some missing money than having Knight vote on Monday.

He turned and headed for the office he kept here in his home. It was far past the time he would normally be in bed, but he knew without a doubt there would be no sleeping tonight. He had to figure a way to cover his tracks with the money.

And then spend the rest of the night worrying about the thousand things that might go wrong.

CHAPTER ELEVEN

Saturday, April 8th
11:30 p.m.

DANNY OPENED THE door for the man and stepped back into his hotel room. All day he had been simply walking through the motions. He had managed to play decent golf, but that had been mostly because he hadn't cared. He kept thinking about his wife. He couldn't imagine what they were doing to her, and yet he couldn't think of anything at all to do. If he told someone, they would kill her, he had no doubt. And he couldn't live with that.

But he was also starting to wonder if he could live with the Senator getting hurt.

"Nice to see you not bein' guarded, kid," the man said. "Lot of cops around here. You have anything to do with that?'

Danny suddenly felt his stomach clamp down into a tight knot. "No!" he said as firmly as he could. "I didn't say a word to anyone."

The guy nodded. "You sure about that?"

"You said you'd kill my wife," Danny said, staring into the dark eyes of the man. "Why would I chance that?"

The guy looked at him for a minute, then nodded. "Smart kid. I believe you. Besides, we've been keepin' an eye on you and I doubt you had a chance to tell anyone."

Danny felt the relief flood over him. "Can I talk to Steph?"

He had insisted that before he would do anything for them, he could talk to Steph every night. The kidnappers had agreed.

"Sure thing, kid," the guy said. He reached into his coat pocket and flipped Danny a cell phone. "Just hit redial."

He did as the man told him to do, then listened as it rang on the other end twice before Steph answered. "Danny?"

"Steph?" he said, the relief he felt flooding through him, making his knees weak and his eyes water.

"Are you all right, Danny?" she asked, her voice barely able to sustain the question.

"I'm fine," he managed to say. "How are they treating you?"

"They're keeping me locked in a bathroom," she said, "but they are feeding me and they haven't touched me."

"I love you," he said.

"I love you, too," she said.

The phone went dead.

He handed the cell phone back to the guy and he put it in his pocket. "You want to see that wonderful wife of yours again, you'll play along tomorrow."

"I'll do what you asked," Danny said.

"Good," the guy said, patting Danny on the shoulder as he headed for the door. "Then I'll see you tomorrow evening for the grand reunion with your wife."

Danny could only nod as the man opened the door, glanced in both directions, and then turned toward the elevators.

The door banged closed.

In all his life Danny had never felt so alone as he did right at that moment.

He stared at the closed door for the longest time before returning to the couch to try to watch television.

It was going to be another long, sleepless night.

A very lonely night.

CHAPTER TWELVE

Sunday, April 9th
6:00 a.m.

THE WAKE-UP CALL and the sun behind the pulled drapes came way, way too early, as far as Bonnie was concerned.

Craig grabbed the phone, listened for a moment, hung it back up, and then just lay beside her half-snoring, half-moaning.

She had the alarm clock set to go off ten minutes after the wake-up call, and if she had anything to do with it, she was going to make sure she used those ten minutes to get as much sleep as she could.

But the wake-up call stirred the memories of what had happened yesterday, and last night.

After the second trip to the cart shed and the discovery of the stairs up into the service area, she and Craig, along with Maxwell and Hagar, had spent two hours planning the protection of the Senator today. Hagar was going to bring in an extra three men, and Maxwell would also have extra men on duty, but he never said how many.

Bonnie never expected to meet any of them. More than likely, knowing how efficient Maxwell had been so far, those extra men would be posing as staff, or even playing in the group ahead of the Senator.

By the time midnight had come around, they had ways figured to keep the Senator completely covered from the moment he left his room to the moment he got on the plane headed for Washington. And as Maxwell assured them, even beyond. Even the plane he was due to fly on would be double-checked and all baggage scanned with special equipment.

Bonnie lay there, letting the conversations from last night go through her mind as Craig snored lightly beside her.

Maxwell had told them he had an idea as to who might want Senator Knight hurt. He had gone on to describe Charles Robins and the relationship between Robins and Senator Knight, including the vote on Monday in Washington in the Senator's committee that would surely cripple Robins' companies. The two men had never met, but were deadly enemies.

"Robins has enough at risk to hurt a United States Senator to stop it?" Bonnie had asked.

"More than enough," Maxwell had replied. "But we don't know for sure that he is behind anything. It could be literally anyone."

"Or that anything is even going to happen," Craig had reminded them. "We're still only acting on what we overheard by accident."

"Which is why we can only protect the Senator and see if anyone makes a move," Maxwell had said.

None of them liked that option, but there just wasn't any other plan as far as they could figure.

Now Bonnie lay in the bed waiting for the alarm to go off, listening to Craig snore, trying not to think about what the day might bring. There wasn't going to be any more sleeping for her, that was for sure. And if she couldn't sleep, Craig shouldn't be able to either.

She flicked off the alarm and rolled over to cuddle with him, putting her naked body the entire length of his back. His skin felt wonderful against hers, firm and smooth and warm.

She rubbed her hand over his unshaven face and then down his chest.

He moaned softly and then rolled toward her and onto his back.

She pushed the covers back so she could see what she was doing in the early morning light coming through the curtains. He didn't move or open his eyes.

She wondered how long he could stay still with her against him. As it turned out, not long. He nuzzled his chin into her neck, letting his unshaven stubble brush lightly against the sensitive area under her ear. The motion sent shivers down her spine and she pushed against him.

Their parking in the cart garage last night had been rudely interrupted and they had been too tired by the time they got back to the room to even think about finishing. But this morning was another matter.

Just the thought of what they had started last night in the cart got her even more excited.

She glanced at the clock. They didn't have much time if they were going to meet Hagar for breakfast.

But they had enough.

CHAPTER THIRTEEN

Sunday, April 9ᵗʰ
7:02 a.m.

BREAKFAST WITH HAGAR was quick, without much talk about what was going on that day with the Senator since they were in a public restaurant with a hundred other golfers. All Hagar had said was that his men were in place and ready. And that he just hoped like hell this was all going to be just a walk in the sun.

Craig agreed completely.

After freezing for the first hour yesterday, Craig brought a jacket and his gloves this morning. Bonnie had done the same, putting on a jacket and lined rain pants over her shorts, swearing she would never get as cold as she had been yesterday again.

Even with the jacket, Craig felt it was almost as cold. And when they reached their cart, they discovered they were riding together. The Senator's cart was already gone.

"I wonder why our cart assignments were switched?" Bonnie asked.

Craig only shrugged as he dropped down onto the cold seat behind the wheel. "Disappointed you have to ride with your husband?"

"When I can ride with a cute, older, and very powerful United States Senator?" Bonnie asked, smiling at him. "Of course."

She sat down next to him and put her hand in his lap. "But on the bright side," she said, "I can do this all day."

Craig laughed. "Just wait until it warms up and we get out behind some of those rocks on the back side. You'll see some groping then."

"Oh," she said, giving his crotch a squeeze as he turned the cart toward the driving range. "I can hardly wait."

"Neither can Hagar and Maxwell's men. We could put a show on for them."

"Sometimes you just take all the fun out of things," she said, pretending to pout, but not taking her hand from his crotch.

"I don't remember taking anything out of anything earlier this morning."

She just laughed and kept squeezing his crotch all the way to the driving range.

By the third hole Craig had shed his jacket.

By the fourth hole Bonnie was down to her tight yellow shorts and white blouse, getting a whistle of appreciation from the Senator that made her blush again. Craig loved the fact that he had a beautiful and smart wife. Sometimes he worried that she was going to leave him for someone better, but at times like today he just enjoyed her beauty and the fact that other men found her beautiful as well.

Actually, it turned out that riding together in the cart behind the Senator and Danny was more fun for Craig. He and Bonnie pointed out Maxwell and Hagar's men to each other, and between them could keep a pretty close eye on the Senator at all times. They made sure that one of them was always standing beside him on every green and tee box.

Plus every time Craig had a chance he touched her and she touched him. By the time this was all over he was going to be hot in more ways than just the temperature.

Craig felt as if they had passed a milestone when they reached the mountain-top tee for the sixteenth hole. Two more holes after this one and a quick lunch and the Senator would be on the way to the airport, out of his and Bonnie's vacation. He had come down here to play golf, spend time with Bonnie and get away from police work. Even though they had had fun so far, it would be nice to have at least one night to not think about life and death situations and protecting a United States Senator.

Just three more holes.

Craig grabbed a five iron and moved up to stand beside Bonnie and the Senator on the top-most tee box. This hole was so beautiful, he just wanted to stand and stare at the valley and mountains below them. The golf course architect had outdone himself when picking this tee box and putting the green down across the canyon. It would be a golf hole Craig would never forget. And one that would be impossible to describe to his friends back in Seattle.

Danny was up first and with his beautiful swing lofted a short iron into the air that floated seemingly forever before landing on the green pretty close to where his ball had been yesterday. Craig would be happy just to have his shot from yesterday again. It was his best of the tournament so far.

The Senator was up next and hit his first shot into the canyon that cut across in front of the green. Disgusted, he dropped another ball. "I'm going to get one over if I have to use every ball in my damned bag."

Bonnie laughed. "I've got an extra dozen you can use as well."

The Senator frowned at her joke. "Just watch this, young lady."

His next shot got into the air and for a moment Craig thought it just might make it over after all, but then it came down

with a resounding smack right square in the middle of the wooden cart bridge that crossed the canyon near the right front of the green.

"Bulls-eye!" Bonnie yelled.

The ball bounced a good fifty feet into the air, and as they all watched open-mouthed, landed on the green and rolled up closer to the pin than Danny's ball.

Hagar and an FBI agent standing on the hillside behind the green applauded that shot, laughing and shaking their heads. Craig almost choked from the laughter, and Bonnie turned red trying to not laugh too hard.

The Senator, who was also laughing, seemed extraordinarily proud of himself. He picked up his tee and turned, a massive smile on his face. "I won't be needing those extra balls, thank you, young lady."

That broke them all up again. Craig shook the Senator's hand and Bonnie gave him a peck on the cheek before moving up to the tee. That shot was going to clearly be the highlight of all their rounds.

Bonnie proceeded to hit three into the canyon before she quit in disgust and with much teasing from the Senator about him lending her golf balls.

Craig managed to get his shot over, but barely, landing it in a pile of rocks far to the left of the green. Two shots in two days over the canyon. He was very proud of himself.

They were getting into the carts, still laughing and joking about the Senator's bridge shot, when suddenly Bonnie grabbed Craig's arm and whispered to him. "What if those two men weren't just passing through the cart shed last night?"

She pointed at the warning signs for the steep cart path they had to wind their

Now Available
from all your favorite booksellers
in trade paper and electronic editions.

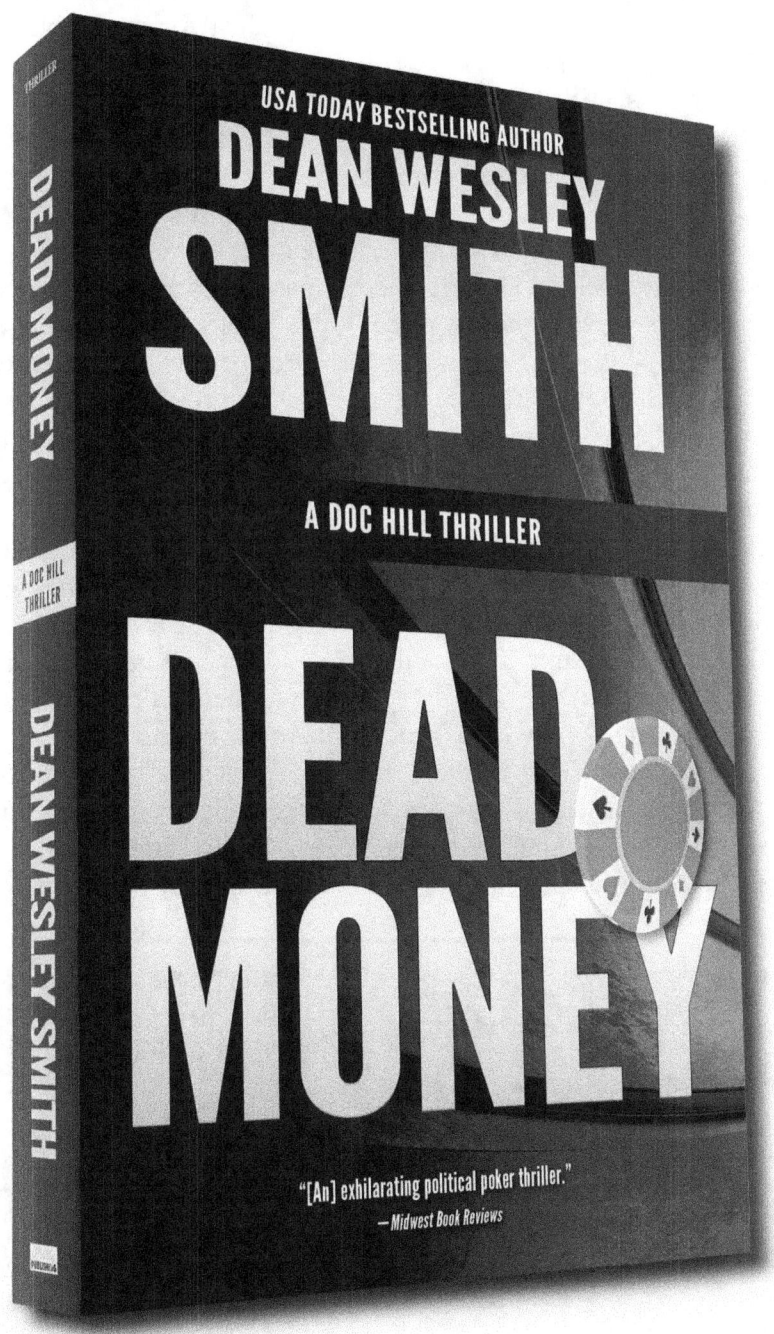

way down. Who knew what would happen if the brakes failed on a cart on the way down this cliff face. Nothing good, that was for sure.

"Senator!" Bonnie shouted before the Senator could start off. He glanced back.

"Can we talk with you for a moment?" Craig asked.

The Senator was still smiling from his shot, but when he saw the frown on Craig's face, he nodded and climbed out of the cart to come back to them.

Maxwell, who had had been sitting in a cart just a few yards behind Bonnie and Craig, came up to see what they wanted as well.

Craig watched the Senator as he came back. Danny glanced around, clearly sweating, then turned back to stare over the valley below.

The little voice in Craig's head said Danny's reaction seemed odd.

Very odd.

Maxwell reached Craig's side at the same time the Senator did.

"What's going on?" Maxwell asked.

Bonnie leaned over Craig in the cart to whisper to both of them. "I just realized that maybe those two men last night might have been in that cart shed for a

reason. I remember hearing the sound of metal clanging on the concrete just a moment before we saw them."

"A tool?" Maxwell asked.

"Maybe," Craig said. "Did your men check the Senator's cart?"

"Just for explosives," Maxwell said, nodding and glancing at the hill in front of them.

"That's good to know," the Senator said, shaking his head at the thought of a bomb in his golf cart. "But I can tell you that the brakes have been working great on that cart. I'm sure it will make it down this."

"Let's let Danny take it just to make sure," Craig said. "Humor us, Senator."

"I agree," Maxwell said.

The Senator chuckled. "I suppose after that shot, I could use a little walk. At least it's downhill."

"I'll walk with you," Bonnie said, climbing out of the cart and moving around the cart to stand beside the Senator.

Maxwell nodded, turned, and moved up to the lead cart. "Danny, go ahead and take the cart to the green."

"But what about the Senator?" Danny asked, clearly sweating now.

Craig stared at the young pro and could clearly see the slight panic hidden

just below the surface. Craig knew that look. He knew it from watching hundreds of criminals get caught in the act. Was it possible that Danny was in on the plan to hurt the Senator?

Maxwell glanced back at Craig. Clearly he had seen the same thing.

"The Senator feels like a walk," Maxwell said.

"That's a long ways, Senator," Danny said, clearly trying to get the Senator in the cart.

"Not with a beautiful woman it isn't," the Senator said, not seeming to notice Danny's discomfort.

"Go ahead," Maxwell said, patting the roof of Danny's cart as the young man reluctantly slid over into the driver's seat. "We'll meet you at the green."

Danny started off, going extra slow.

"Stay with the Senator," Craig whispered to Maxwell. "I'll follow Danny."

Maxwell nodded and quickly turned and spoke softly into a communications device he had in his watch. Craig saw one of the men on the far hill behind the green start down toward the green at once, with Hagar following.

Craig stayed a good twenty paces behind Danny as they went across the cliff face under the tee box and made the first switchback. Twice the kid looked over his shoulder at Craig with a very frightened look.

Craig only smiled.

Clearly the kid knew something, or was very, very afraid of driving a golf cart.

Craig was betting on the kid knowing something.

After the next switchback the cart path took a sharp drop as it crossed the steepest part of the cliff, then made another switchback seemingly out over space.

It was the scariest corner on the hill and the most dangerous. There were warning signs to use brakes and watch speed, and there were bumps built into the path to remind any driver to keep the cart's speed down. On this cliff face, Craig couldn't imagine any golfer trying to go fast on purpose.

Or forgetting, for that matter.

Ahead of Craig there was a slight pop from the Senator's cart and Danny looked suddenly panicked.

Danny's cart seemed to shoot ahead, as if Danny had put his foot on the gas.

On a downhill slope most golf carts have inhibitors that slowed the cart if it got going too fast.

Danny's clearly did not, or was suddenly broken.

Danny was almost smashing his head on the roof as the cart banged over the warning bumps. He seemed frozen in panic, holding the wheel with both hands, his arms straight ahead.

The cart was heading into the switchback far, far too fast. It would never make it. Craig instantly knew what the plan had been.

With the Senator driving and on the cliff side, there would have been no chance for him to get out with Danny beside him. But there was no one blocking Danny.

"Jump!" Craig shouted.

Danny dove across the seat and out the passenger side at the last possible instant, just as the cart tipped toward the driver's side and went over the rock edge.

Somehow Danny managed to clear the cart, rolling once on the pavement and coming up hard against a rock with a sickening thud.

The cart, with the two sets of clubs rattling and banging, rolled over and over down the steep rock face, filling the valley with a smashing sound that echoed off the rock hills.

Clubs flew everywhere as the cart gathered speed end-over-end. The top of the cart ripped away like paper, spinning in the air. A couple of the heavy batteries under the seat flew away like large missiles.

Danny's massive golf bag came loose and did three end-over-end flips, scattering clubs and gear everywhere.

Fiberglass from the cart's side panel exploded in fragments as it smashed into a massive rock.

What was left of the cart finally did a quick flip and disappeared over the cliff face and into the deep canyon in front of the green. The sound of it smashing into the rocks and brush at the bottom was like nothing Craig had ever heard.

The echo of the sound took a long time to die off.

If the Senator had been in that cart, he could have easily been killed in the "accident."

Craig had his cart stopped and was bending over Danny as the young pro groaned and sat up. He was going to be bruised and scraped, but it didn't look like anything was broken.

"Don't move," Craig said.

Danny ignored him and tried to stand.

"I said don't move!"

"But I have—"

Craig flipped the kid over on his face on the cart path and pulled his arm behind it, leaning on the arm and Danny's back with one knee.

"You struggle and I break the arm," Craig said, using his weight to hold the younger man down. He wasn't going to take any chances with someone who could try to kill a Senator.

Danny spit out some gravel and blood. "Why are you doing this to me?"

"You know as well as I do," Craig said, pushing down even harder on the arm, making Danny jerk in pain and scrape the side of his face on the hot concrete path.

Craig glanced around. Both Hagar and the agent who had been behind the green were heading at a run up the cart path toward him. The agent was going to beat the local detective, but not by much. Maxwell was coming down the trail in a cart, going as fast as he dared. The Senator and Bonnie were out of sight up near the tee box.

"You're not going to be playing much golf where you're going," Craig said to Danny, pushing a little more on the arm and back with his knee. "Attempted murder of a United States Senator should get you about fifty years."

"But I didn't—"

Craig pressed down on Danny's arm just a little harder with his knee, cutting off the kid's excuse in a gasp of pain.

"The FBI guys are almost here," Craig said. "As a suggestion, I would recommend very highly you tell them everything. You might just get out in time to make the Seniors' tour if you do that. Maybe even earlier."

"You don't understand," Danny said, clearly on the edge of tears. "I had to. My wife. You don't understand."

Now the wife comment shocked Craig. He was about to ask another question when Maxwell slid the cart to a stop behind the one Craig had been in. At the same moment the agent from behind the green, clearly out of breath and sweating from the hard run in the heat, came around the switchback where the Senator's cart had gone over.

"Is he all right?" Maxwell asked as Craig got off the young pro and yanked Danny to his feet.

"For someone who's going to spend a large part of his youth in jail," Craig said, "I think so. Better read him his rights for attempted murder and whatever else you might want to add on. I think he might have a few things to say."

Maxwell nodded for the other agent to take Danny and do just that.

"Wait," Danny said. "I can get you who's behind this, but you have to save my wife."

Craig looked at Maxwell. Clearly Maxwell was just as puzzled as Craig was.

"Read him his rights," Maxwell said, "And then we'll talk."

Then into his communications watch Maxwell said, "Get the Senator down here and hidden in the canyon. Quick. And block entrances to this area from both sides. I want a medical evacuation helicopter here as quickly as possible, and a secure room ready in the hospital."

Craig was impressed. Maxwell was thinking clearly and quickly.

"The Senator went over in the cart, I assume," Craig said, smiling at Maxwell who was staring down the hill at the scattered clubs, parts of a cart roof, and Danny's almost empty bag.

"He had an accident, as far as the world is going to know tonight," Maxwell said.

At that point Hagar made it up the final stretch looking white and out of breath. Running up a steep hill in desert heat could hurt anyone. It clearly hadn't done Hagar any good.

Maxwell stepped over to Danny who was finished having his rights read to him by a still-out-of-breath and sweating agent. "So how can you help us?"

"I'm supposed to meet the man who kidnapped my wife tonight in my room at

nine, if the Senator can't make the flight to Washington. And they will release her then."

"Release your wife?"

"They took her on Friday," Danny said, panic in his eyes. He had blood dripping down the side of his face and one leg looked like it had been scraped with sandpaper, but he wasn't seeming to notice. "They said they wanted to make sure I would help. If I didn't, or told the police, they were going to kill her and me."

Maxwell nodded. "So why did you go ahead and wreck the cart without the Senator in it?"

"I didn't do that," Danny said. "The brakes failed like they were supposed to. I was just insurance, to make sure that if the brakes didn't fail, I made the cart go over the edge with the Senator in it. But don't you see, I had to, to save my wife."

Craig shook his head. "You and your wife would have never lived to see your home again."

Danny looked even paler than he had a moment before.

Maxwell nodded. "People who would do this can't leave witnesses."

Maxwell glanced back up the cart path. Then to the agent Maxwell pointed at the spot where the cart path became very steep. "Sweep that hillside for a buried transmitter. I bet we'll find a matching one inside the braking system of the cart."

Craig glanced down the cliff face. "If there's anything left of the cart."

Maxwell glanced down the hill. "There'll be enough. Let's just hope they were stupid enough to leave us some prints as well."

"Oh, my," the Senator said as he and Bonnie and another agent came down the path. "Danny, are you all right?"

"I'm so sorry, Senator," Danny said. Then he dropped to the path and broke into sobs.

"Danny?" the Senator said, clearly shocked as he stared at the young pro, then at Craig and Maxwell.

Craig stepped toward Bonnie and the Senator. Bonnie gave him a quick hug.

"It seems Danny was blackmailed into helping them," Craig said. "And I'm afraid, Senator, that you're not going to get a chance to make that birdie putt."

The Senator glanced down over the edge of the cart path at the scattered clubs and parts of a cart on the steep, rocky cliff, clearly understanding how close he had just come to being hurt or killed. "I doubt my putter survived that crash anyway."

"Senator," Maxwell said, "we need you down near the canyon so we can airlift you out. Just in case the wrong people end up watching."

"I'm going to the hospital, huh?" the Senator asked, clearly understanding the plan.

"Actually, yes," Maxwell said. "And then directly to the airport where you'll catch a flight to Washington under complete secrecy."

"Sounds like a plan," he said to Maxwell. "Good luck catching whoever is behind this."

"We'll have a report to you tomorrow," Maxwell said. "We only have to keep the charade up for the night."

The Senator nodded, then turned to Bonnie and Craig. "I don't know even where to start thanking you."

He shook Craig's hand firmly, then Bonnie gave him a kiss.

"It's been our pleasure, Senator," Bonnie said. "Thirty-three of the most enjoyable holes of golf I have ever played."

The Senator laughed and stepped back and looked at Bonnie's tight shorts and white blouse. "Young lady, trust me, it has been my pleasure as well."

With a laugh at Bonnie's blushing red face, the Senator winked at Craig and turned and headed down the cart path.

All Craig could do was chuckle at his beautiful wife.

Twelve minutes later the Senator was airlifted out on a stretcher, headed for the hospital and his home in Washington.

CHAPTER FOURTEEN

Sunday, April 9th
2:36 p.m.

BONNIE SAT ON the bed with Craig in a room on the hotel's top floor and watched as the last of Danny's scrapes were treated.

Clearly Maxwell and the other FBI agents had been using this room as a base. It was bigger than her and Craig's room, yet considerably smaller than the Senator's massive suite. From the looks of the table and kitchen area, a number of agents had been going and coming from here twenty-fours hours a day. Right now Maxwell and three agents were here, as well as Hagar and Danny. The agent working on Danny's cuts and scrapes clearly had a good knowledge of first aid.

After the Senator was airlifted away, they had decided that to get Danny back into the hotel without arousing suspicion, she and Craig would walk him in. It would be logical that if he wasn't under suspicion for any crime, that he would be with his playing companions.

As Danny was being treated, he told what had happened to him and his wife over the last week. To Bonnie the story he told had a ring of truth through it. But on top of that, she wanted to believe him. Craig was clearly not so sure.

It seemed that on Friday morning, while Danny was at his golf course for a few hours, Danny's wife, Steph, was taken from their apartment in Sedona. Danny guessed that there had been three, but by the time he got home only one was waiting for him. Danny had seen the man who wasn't masked a few times this weekend around the hotel, and the guy had come to Danny's room last night.

Danny said he had told the man that he wouldn't cooperate unless he could have proof his wife was alive every day. Danny looked up at Maxwell. "They threatened to kill her, but I held to my demand."

Maxwell nodded. "Go on. What did they do then?"

"They let me talk to her for a few seconds Friday night late, and again last night," he said, barely holding it together.

Craig glanced at Maxwell. Bonnie knew exactly what Craig was thinking. If there were phone calls, there could be traces on those calls. Maxwell nodded, clearly thinking along the same lines.

He turned to one of three agents standing nearby. "Get Danny's room and home phone records and get those calls traced."

"They weren't on my room phone," Danny said. "The guy always handed me a cell phone and told me to punch redial."

"Damn," Maxwell said.

"How about the face of the phone?" Bonnie asked. "Could you see the number?"

Now Available
from all your favorite booksellers
in trade paper and electronic editions.

Danny shook his head. "The guy had it taped over."

"Smart," Hagar said.

Bonnie had to agree.

"It was so hard," Danny said, "not calling the police."

"You should have, you know," Maxwell said.

"I do now," Danny said softly. "But I was so afraid they were going to kill her."

Bonnie had no doubt not calling the police was going to be one decision Danny would regret for a long time. But now wasn't the time to dwell on that.

"What did they say was going to happen?" Craig asked.

"That an accident was going to hurt the Senator during the golf tournament today, and I was to make sure the accident happened no matter what.

"Did they say what kind of accident?" Maxwell asked.

"Just a cart accident on a steep hill," Danny said. "When I saw the 16th hole yesterday I knew that was where it would happen. They said if the Senator was too injured to get on the plane, my wife would be released tonight. If not, I would never see her again. And they would make sure I never saw anyone again."

"Get on the plane?" Hagar asked, stepping closer to Danny. "You sure he used those exact words?"

Bonnie had been just about to ask that same question, but Hagar beat her to it. That detail had to be an important part of finding who was behind this.

Danny nodded at Hagar. "That's what he said."

"The vote tomorrow against Charles Robins' companies?" Craig asked Maxwell.

"Sure seems that way," Maxwell said. "We've had the Robins' estate under surveillance since the accident."

There was a silence in the room.

"Okay, what time are you to meet your contact?" Maxwell asked.

"Six, in my room," Danny said.

"It's four now," Hagar said, glancing at his watch.

"Okay, we need to get you down there and set up," Maxwell said. "We want to catch your contact to find out where they are keeping your wife. And who they are working for."

"That's going to be a problem," Bonnie said. "What happens if someone is watching? Danny can't go into this meeting alone, but going into his room with one of your agents might stop the entire thing."

"I agree," Hagar said. "These people were sophisticated enough to blow the brakes on a golf cart at the right point, it would be easy for them to be watching Danny's room."

"Maybe even have it bugged, just in case," Craig said.

Bonnie couldn't agree more.

"My room's been bugged?" Danny asked, clearly trying to keep up with all this.

"In all likelihood that's exactly right," Maxwell said.

"How about Craig and I go to Danny's room with him," Bonnie said, "stage a leaving, and hide out in the room until Danny's contact shows up."

Maxwell nodded. "Might work. We can have you all wired and we can be staged in rooms in both directions down the hall to block any retreat."

"If we're not going to take a chance of being seen," Craig said, "I don't see any other choice."

Neither did she.

Just under one hour later she and Craig were walking with Danny from the elevator to his room, not really talking. Bonnie could feel the heaviness of the police-issue pistol against the small of her back, its metal cool in the air-conditioned hotel. It was the only place on her they could find to hide it safely. Craig had his tucked in the side of his belt and his golf shirt pulled out to cover it.

Danny had memorized a few lines, and understood completely that he wasn't to talk to Craig and Bonnie after they said good-bye just inside his room.

She and Craig were going to station themselves inside Danny's bedroom in the small suite. The moment Danny's contact was let into the suite, Hagar and Maxwell and their people would be outside the door, ready to come through within ten seconds.

A very long ten seconds, as far as Bonnie was concerned. While Danny was in the bathroom getting ready to go, Maxwell had told Bonnie and Craig and Hagar that he suspected that the contact wasn't there for information about the Senator, but to kill Danny.

Maxwell figured they were going to have to move fast.

The plan was that Danny was to let the man into the room, and close the door, giving Maxwell and Hagar enough time to get into position before coming through. When Bonnie and Craig heard Maxwell break in, they were to come in from the bedroom. At that moment Danny was to drop to the floor and stay there.

It was a sound plan, but Bonnie had a fear it wasn't going to work like they hoped. She didn't know why she felt that way. More than likely just jitters.

It had been a long time, since she had been involved in something like this. And then only once in her second year

on the force. This was much more of what Craig did in his job as a detective. She very seldom had to stage raids on homes of domestically abused children. Usually she and her people just went in with a warrant and took the children out. At times it got ugly, but she always had plenty of help.

They reached Danny's room without seeing anyone else in the hallway.

She knew that Hagar and Maxwell and their people had already taken their positions one-at-a-time in rooms along the hall. And more than likely Hagar and Maxwell had just watched the three of them walk by.

Craig and Bonnie were also wired for sound, but Danny wasn't, just in case the first thing the contact did was pat him down.

Danny fumbled with the key card, then managed to get the door open. They all stepped inside and the door closed. The first thing Danny did was move to the windows and draw the curtains in both the living area and the bedroom.

Then as Danny stood with Bonnie near the door, looking scared, Craig, gun drawn, silently and quickly checked out the rooms of the small suite to make sure no one else was in there. When he came out of the bedroom and nodded, Bonnie went into her script. If someone was listening, it needed to be clear to them what was happening.

"Are you sure you're going to be all right?" she asked.

"I think so," Danny said. "Just shaken up."

Bonnie nodded to him that he was doing fine. He looked like he might be sick at any moment.

"Understandable," Craig said. "But it was an accident. Remember that."

"Sure," Danny said, his voice shaking. "Thanks."

"You going to be all right?" Bonnie asked. "You want us to stay with you for a little bit?"

"No, thanks," Danny said, staying with the script they had worked out. "I think I just need to rest."

"All right," Craig said. "We'll meet you for dinner at seven in the restaurant."

"Sounds good," Danny said.

Bonnie opened the door, then let it close a moment later with a loud thump. Her own heart seemed to be pounding even harder and she was sure Maxwell and his people could hear every beat through the microphone taped inside her blouse.

Craig held his finger to his lips in the motion for all of them to be very silent. Then he moved over and turned on the television, putting it on one of the movie channels at a moderate volume.

He pointed to the couch for Danny to sit, then motioned for Bonnie to come with him into the bedroom.

Craig eased the door almost closed behind them, leaving just enough of a crack in the door that he could see Danny sitting like a statue on the couch.

Bonnie glanced around at Danny's clothes from yesterday tossed on the chair, and an unopened Star Trek paperback book on the dresser. Then she glanced at Craig.

He gave her a quick thumbs-up sign.

Now all they had to do was wait.

Silently.

CHAPTER FIFTEEN

Sunday, April 9th
5:31 p.m.

CHARLES ROBINS STARED at the ringing phone for a few moments, then decided he might as well answer it. Last night he hadn't slept much, and all morning he felt as if he was walking in a haze. He could never remember feeling like this before.

The phone that was ringing was a private number known only to a few people. The man working for him today was not one of them, but Charles had no doubt the man knew it.

Charles moved across his lavishly furnished study to the cell phone sitting on the corner of his oak desk. He hadn't asked the man for an update, but somehow he expected one since the extra demand for money. How else was he to know when to pay?

He picked up the phone on the fourth ring and said, "Yes."

The man's distinctive voice filled Charles's mind as if the volume on his phone was turned up high.

"Oh, pardon the interruption," the man said, his voice as level and controlled as always. "I was trying to call the hospital."

The line went dead and Charles put the phone down. He didn't know how he felt. Clearly Senator Knight was in the hospital, the man's mission accomplished as planned. But he wouldn't let just one phone call be his confirmation.

Charles moved over to a wall cabinet and opened it so his large television was exposed. He quickly turned it on and flipped to a local Phoenix news channel. They were covering the Senator's tragic accident, as he would have expected they would. It seemed the Senator's cart had gone out of control on a steep path and rolled down a rocky slope. The Senator had been airlifted to the hospital where his condition was considered critical.

Charles flipped off the television and moved back to his desk. He was feeling even more numb than he had earlier, but he was sure a good night's sleep would solve that problem. And now that his companies were out of immediate danger from the good Senator, he just might get some sleep.

He dropped down into his chair and clicked on his computer screen. He had the money set up to transfer to the man's account after it was confirmed about the Senator. But it wasn't as much as the man had demanded. In fact, it was nowhere near as much.

Charles glanced at the total, then laughed. "You think you can blackmail me, do you?" With a click the funds were transferred to the man's account. "I can change the rules just as easily as you can," Charles said to the man, as if he could hear, "and there isn't a damn thing you can do about it. Not with the security I've got around here. You work for me, remember?"

With a laugh Charles shut down his computer and stood. "A good brandy and a steak for dinner is just what the doctor ordered."

Charles laughed again, starting to feel a lot better. "Probably not the Senator's doctor."

CHAPTER SIXTEEN

Sunday, April 9th
5:47 p.m.

TO CRAIG THE first fifteen minutes of waiting seemed to drag on and on as they stood just inside Danny's bedroom door.

Bonnie paced silently while he leaned against the door frame. Every thirty seconds or so he peeked through the slightly open door to make sure Danny was still sitting on the couch. The young golf pro was, watching television and doing his best to remain still, mostly without success.

But his orders from Maxwell were to stay on the couch, without moving around, until the man showed up, and that was exactly what Danny was doing.

Craig couldn't blame the kid for squirming and worrying. He was in a situation different from anything he had ever seen outside a movie. And his wife had been taken hostage all because of someone's desire to get to a United States Senator. How completely unfair was that?

If that was what had really happened.

At first Craig hadn't believed the kid, but over the last hour he had started to. Craig's biggest worry now was that Danny's wife was already dead. There was no doubt that the Senator would be injured or dead and Danny might be facing a death sentence shortly if he and Bonnie hadn't accidentally overheard that conversation the first night. But finding Danny's wife was another matter.

Right now Maxwell and his people were scrambling to triangulate cell calls and track down any lead that might give them a clue to Steph Baines's location.

Bonnie found a hotel note pad on the nightstand beside the phone and scribbled a quick note, holding it up to him to see.

This waiting is driving me nuts!

Craig smiled at her and nodded his agreement. They still had almost thirty minutes before the man Danny was supposed to meet was even scheduled to show.

Craig took the pen and pad and wrote a note back to her.

Me too. Wish we had turned the television on in here as well.

She read his note and nodded. Then took the pad and wrote: *That would have helped.*

They wrote a few notes back and forth for the next ten minutes until suddenly there was a knock on the hall door into Danny's room.

Craig checked on Danny through the crack in the open door. The young pro was staring his way, a very frightened look on his face.

Craig silently opened the bedroom door enough for Danny to see him and motioned for Danny to go ahead and let his contact into the suite.

Danny took a deep breath and went for the door as Craig eased the bedroom door closed and pulled his gun, quickly checking it to make sure it was loaded and ready to fire.

Bonnie had her gun in her hand as well. Her face was flushed and she was fighting to control her breathing. That knock must have really startled her.

It startled him, that was for sure, even though that was what they had been waiting for.

He motioned for her to take a position on the far side of the dresser behind where the door would open.

Craig then moved over against the wall by the closet so he would have a clear angle at the doorway. If the guy checked in here before Maxwell and Hagar came in, Craig planned on greeting the guy with a loaded gun, and he wanted Bonnie flanking the man, but not in his line of fire.

Also he and Bonnie had worked out that if they had to go through the door, he would go first and to his left, she second and to the right. These starting positions would make it easier for that to happen.

Bonnie got into position and nodded she was ready.

"Yeah," Danny said as he opened the doorway into the hall.

A very long pause.

Craig glanced at Bonnie and motioned that she should take a deep breath. She did, silently, then mouthed to him to be careful.

"I see our Senator had himself a little accident, as planned," a man's voice said as the door to the hall closed.

Craig glanced at Bonnie, whose eyes were wide. She recognized the voice as well as he did. It was one of the guys they had overheard on Friday night.

"My wife?" Danny asked. "Is she all right?"

"Ahh, sure thing, kid," the man said. "Right as rain. You and her can be doing the humpy-bumpy tonight."

"So when can I talk to her?" Danny demanded.

Craig glanced at his watch. Thirteen seconds had gone by. Maxwell and Hagar should be coming through the door at any instant.

"I'm goin' to take you to a place where you can talk to her," the man said.

Craig knew that the place the man wanted to take Danny to was where Danny would be killed.

"No!" Danny said. "I want to talk to her now!"

Craig glanced at Bonnie, whose eyes were round. That wasn't in Danny's script.

"Sure, kid," the man said. "No skin off my nose."

Craig could hear the beeping of a cell phone as the man dialed a number. If he was actually dialing the location of Danny's wife, Craig hoped Maxwell and the others were listening and would give the call time to happen. That way they had something to triangulate to find the location.

"Put the kid's wife on the phone again," the man said.

Then Danny said, "Steph? Are you all right?"

There was a pause.

"I love you," Danny said.

"That's enough, kid," the man said. "You'll see her soon enough.

There was a clear sound of the cell phone cover being snapped shut. "Now, let's go."

At that instant the door from the hall burst open and Maxwell's voice shouted "FBI!"

Craig took one step toward the bedroom door and yanked it open, moving left, his gun aimed at the man standing near the television. The guy looked to be no more than thirty and couldn't have been taller than five-foot-five.

Danny dove away from the man for the couch, rolling over a coffee table as he went.

The man drew a revolver from under his coat jacket, spinning at Maxwell coming through the hallway door.

"Don't!" Craig shouted.

"Drop the gun!" Maxwell shouted.

The guy didn't listen.

It was a very stupid thing not to do.

The guy had his gun out and was turning on Maxwell when both Craig and Maxwell fired.

The two shots slammed the room in sound.

Craig was aiming at the man's shoulder and arm. From fifteen feet, he knew he didn't miss.

Maxwell was even closer and clearly didn't miss either.

The man spun around like someone had put a boogie-board under his feet and yanked on him. His gun banged against the wall from the force of the impacts and ended up near the small bar.

The man did a complete three hundred and sixty degree turn and smashed to the floor, face up, staring at the ceiling, his legs twisted under him.

The noise inside the small room was deafening from the two shots and the air stank of gunpowder. Craig had had to fire his gun in a few enclosed areas before, and the intensity of the explosion and smell always caught him by surprise.

Both Craig and Maxwell were over the man before he even stopped falling. Craig could see that the guy had been hit twice. Once in the right shoulder, which was Craig's shot, and once in the stomach, which had to be Maxwell's. The guy clearly wasn't going anywhere. He was going to be lucky to live.

Now the copperish odor of blood filled the air, mixing with the gunpowder smell as blood stained the carpet black below the guy.

Maxwell bent down over the man, whose eyes were fluttering like he had sand in them.

Craig glanced around at Bonnie, who was standing over Danny, her hand on his shoulder as he sobbed into the couch. Two other agents and Hagar were also in the room.

"Ambulance," Craig said and Hagar grabbed the phone off the stand beside him.

"And get the number of that last call and its location," Maxwell said, picking the cell phone out of the man's front pocket and tossing it to one of the agents. "Stat!"

The agent with the phone grabbed it out of the air, jumped toward the door, and disappeared into the hall.

"Who hired you?" Maxwell asked, turning back to the man on the floor.

The guy stopped blinking long enough to look at Maxwell, then at Craig.

Craig knew the look. It was an awareness of death coming, as if suddenly a person knew death now and accepted it all in one instant. Craig had seen it on every death he had witnessed. The guy had the look now.

"Come on," Maxwell said, urgency in his voice. "Who hired you?"

The guy looked like he wanted to say something.

The silence as they tried to listen for what the man would say seemed extra intense in the room after the sound of shots.

But there was going to be nothing but silence.

All that came out of the guy's mouth were a few bloody bubbles before he died.

CHAPTER SEVENTEEN

Sunday, April 9th
7:01 p.m.

BONNIE HAD BEEN a cop long enough to see her share of death. And every time she hoped she would never have to see more.

This time was no different.

Just easier.

The deaths of children and teenagers were the ones that bothered her the most, but every death seemed to carve a small chunk out of her soul, leaving her feeling just a little more empty and a little more jaded toward life and people.

Having the guy die in the fight in the hotel room was startling, and disturbing, but for some reason she didn't find herself that upset about it. He had tried to kill Senator Knight, had kidnapped Danny's wife, and was more than likely going to kill Danny and his wife if they had given him time.

Having him die wasn't a great loss to the world, the way she figured it. She knew that was cold, but sometimes being a cop made you cold when it came to scum.

Craig clearly felt the same way. Craig seemed more upset that he was going to have to do massive paperwork and attend post-shooting hearings after all this was over. Hagar had promised him he would help speed the process. And if he did have to come back for a hearing, just think of the golf he could play. That comment had cheered Craig up some.

Right now she and Craig and the rest were much more worried about getting

Danny's wife recovered safely. The cell phone they had gotten off the dead guy was stolen, and the number called had been to another stolen cell phone.

No surprise there.

Maxwell and his team had managed to get the area the cell call went into narrowed down to a ten-block radius in a Phoenix suburb. But the only way to pinpoint the call exactly to one location was to call the number again.

And somehow keep the line open long enough to get a fix on the location.

With the help of the Scottsdale police, the Phoenix police, and other agencies nearby, they had quietly blocked off the entire ten-block area and were standing ready to swarm in on the location as soon as they had it pinpointed. There was going to be no talking with whoever was holding Danny's wife. They were going to swarm in and take her back without warning.

Danny seemed ready as well to help in getting his wife to safety. They had all gone back up to the FBI's room on the top floor of the hotel, leaving Danny's room for the crime scene people and FBI to go over. Maxwell had figured if Danny made the phone call, there might be more of a chance of it staying connected long enough to get an exact location pinpointed.

Bonnie agreed and was standing beside Danny, with Craig on the other side, when Maxwell said, "Ready."

Danny nodded and pressed redial on the dead man's cell phone. Then he carefully put it to his ear as if he was afraid it might explode on him.

Bonnie forced herself to let out the breath she was holding and put her hand gently on Danny's shoulder to let him know they were there for him.

After a short moment Danny said, "The guy said I could talk to my wife again."

A slight pause.

Danny looked panicked.

"He's right here," Danny said. "Just put my wife on."

Behind Danny, Maxwell signaled thumbs up.

They had the location and were closing in. But he wanted Danny to keep talking if he could. It would be better for those moving in to keep the guy on the line and busy somehow.

"All right, all right," Danny said. "You can talk to him. Then let me talk to my wife again will ya?"

Bonnie was impressed at the young pro. He had played it perfectly.

Danny glanced at Bonnie with the phone held out in front of him. He had the questioning look of what was he supposed to do now? He had gone through all his lines they had worked on and he clearly wasn't capable of making something up in his state of mind.

Craig motioned for Danny to talk into the phone again, but Bonnie could tell Danny was clearly about to lose it. This was all far, far beyond his depth.

Bonnie shook her head at her husband, signaling him to not push the young pro any more.

Craig glanced at Maxwell, then took the phone. He smiled at her and gave her his nothing-to-lose-shrug.

She agreed. They had pinpointed the location and at this point they had nothing to lose and everything to gain by keeping whoever was on the other end of the line busy for just a few more seconds.

"Let him talk to his wife, fer cryin' out loud," Craig said.

Bonnie was impressed. Craig's voice sounded like a passable imitation of the dead man's voice. Sometimes her husband's hidden skills were just amazing.

"Yeah, yeah, I know," Craig said after a short moment, "but the kid wouldn't budge without another call."

Suddenly Craig held the phone away from his ear. Bonnie could hear the sounds of gunfire coming from the phone. One shot, another two quick ones, then nothing.

Craig carefully put the cell phone back up to his ear and listened for a moment, then shook his head that there was nothing on the other end.

They all looked at Maxwell.

"Is Steph all right?" Danny asked Maxwell.

He said nothing.

Bonnie could feel her stomach clamping down hard as she waited. Beside her Danny seemed as if he might just faint from the fear and worry and waiting.

Maxwell was listening to reports from his people on headphones. Suddenly he broke into a big smile at Danny. "They have her."

"She's all right?" Danny asked, his voice weak and shaking.

"She's all right," Maxwell said, smiling the broadest grin Bonnie could have imagined the man smiling. "They're taking her to the hospital. You can meet her there."

At that Danny just slumped into a chair and broke down and started crying.

For a moment the hardened cops and agents in the room looked at the young golf pro with stunned looks.

Then Bonnie sat down beside him and put her arm on his shoulder for comfort. He deserved a good cry.

Around her a lot of men were smiling, including her husband. It looked like this was over for the moment.

And for a change, real life had a happy ending, even if the guy was crying.

CHAPTER EIGHTEEN

Sunday, April 9th
8:37 p.m.

THE MAN CHARLES Robins called Bill signaled for the limo driver to stop in a parking lot as he checked the account balance on his laptop computer screen one more time just to make sure.

It came up the same.

Charles Robins had shorted him exactly a half million dollars on the final payment.

"Stupid idiot," the man said.

He snapped the computer closed and put it back in his case.

Then as he was looking out the window of the limo, he started to laugh. "Stupid men always make stupid mistakes."

He had always known that Charles Robins was a stupid man, so this final act of greed was no surprise. It was mostly luck and underhanded dealings that had allowed Robins to build his house-of-cards fortune. The man had known that before he went to work for Robins. For years he had waited for this exact moment, the exact right opportunity to strike at Robins, take as much of Robins's money as he could, and move on.

He had gotten a half million out of the idiot. And now Robins had made the fatal mistake of not paying the rest. It was time to show Robins that there were some things not even an idiot could buy his way out of.

The man signaled for the driver to start up again, then reached into a brief-case and pulled out a cell phone. It was one of ten stolen for this operation that he hadn't used yet.

He punched in the number for the man he called Benny. The guy was all New York and proud of it. Benny didn't know the man's real name and he didn't know Benny's. They simply helped each other out when help was needed.

The phone rang three times too many without being picked up.

The man instantly clicked off his phone and punched the button for the window beside him to roll down. He used a handkerchief to carefully wipe off his fingerprints from the phone and the keypad. There was a stretch of empty desert and litter a few hundred feet ahead. As the limo went past he tossed the phone into the litter beside the road.

He put the window up and then keyed in the intercom to the driver of the limo. "Turn right at the next corner and then right again at the next and head back into town."

"Understood, sir," the driver said.

He sat back and thought. Was it possible that Benny had just put the phone down? By this time of night he should have already been at the house with Danny the golf pro. And both Danny and his young wife should be dead, if Benny followed orders. He was hoping to make use of the two bodies.

Was it possible that Benny was busy with that chore?

The man nodded and pulled out another cell phone. He punched in another number, this one for the phone of Benny's assistant who had been guarding the young wife.

The phone rang two too many rings before a voice answered. "Yeah."

The voice sounded like Benny's voice, but it wasn't Benny.

He clicked the cell phone closed, quickly wiped it clean of his fingerprints, and tossed it out the window. It bounced under a parked car.

"Driver, take a left at the next corner and go until you reach the freeway. Then head for Tucson."

"Yes, sir," the driver said.

It was clear that Benny and one of his men were either dead or captured by the FBI. It made sense that they would get the young pro to break the moment the Senator had his accident. And from there the trail was easy to Benny and his helper. He was going to miss Benny, that was for sure. A good worker.

But he wasn't going to miss the money he now didn't have to pay Benny. That was an extra bonus.

But what to do about Charles Robins?

The man sat back in the comfort of the limo and sipped a brandy, thinking. He wasn't halfway to Tucson before he came up with a great plan.

CHAPTER NINETEEN

Sunday, April 9th
11:21 p.m.

CRAIG PUSHED AWAY his mostly empty plate and sipped on the Diet Coke. They had been lucky to find a place with food this good so late on a Sunday night. It looked more like a diner stuffed inside an old freight warehouse, but Hagar had sworn by the place and he had been right. Great service, great food, and background music low enough to talk over.

What more could they have asked for?

At the moment Hagar was finishing a large plate of some sort of Mexican food Craig didn't recognize.

Maxwell had already pushed away the last of his barbecue chicken.

Bonnie was trying to polish off the last few pieces of her steak.

Around them there were still people coming in and being seated. Clearly the locals knew this place well. Craig couldn't imagine how busy it was during peak hours if there were this many people here on a late Sunday night.

For all of them it had been one very long day, topped with the scene in the hospital with Danny and Steph getting back together. Just the memory of that made Craig smile. The quiet, sullen young golf pro that they had played golf with all weekend suddenly had become happy, full of life, with a light in his eyes as he and his wife hugged and cried together.

Craig couldn't even imagine playing golf while Bonnie was being held hostage. But Danny had done what he thought he had to do. And somehow had managed. He was one strong kid.

From what Maxwell had said, because of Danny's help getting to some of the men behind the attempt on the Senator's life, and the situation of his wife being kidnapped, no charges against Danny would be brought. He and Steph were just victims of the larger plan.

At the hospital Craig had apologized to Danny for treating him so roughly on the cart path after the accident.

Danny said it was all right. For not calling the police at once he deserved much more than that. Then he had added that he never wanted to ever be on the receiving end of being arrested again by an angry cop. Once was enough.

Initially Craig and Bonnie had been scheduled to fly out early in the morning and be back to work on Tuesday from this so-called vacation. But since Craig had been involved in the shooting of one of the suspects, there were going to be hearings to attend and paperwork to fill out.

Bonnie had called the airline and pushed their flight back to Tuesday. Then she had told their bosses in Seattle what had happened. So with an extra day or so, maybe, just maybe, they could end up having a little time alone.

"So what happens next?" Bonnie asked Maxwell as she gave up and pushed her plate away from her with a few bites of steak still left.

Maxwell shrugged. "Steph Baines said there were three men who kidnapped her. Two are now dead, so we still got one out there somewhere."

"The guy who made the phone calls to the cell phones?" Craig asked.

Craig's attempt to imitate one of the dead men on the second call had failed instantly. Clearly the man making the calls was smart and was being very careful. Both calls had been made from different stolen cell phones, and both phones had been quickly found, obviously tossed out of a moving car.

"More than likely he's the third," Maxwell said, nodding as he sipped a cup of coffee. "And he's now a good distance out of the area."

"But he wasn't the money man," Hagar said.

"I doubt it," Maxwell said. "We're pretty sure that is Robins. He's the only one with motive to hurt the Senator. But proving it without the third man in custody is going to be damned hard."

"Money trail?" Bonnie asked.

"Maybe," Maxwell said. "If we can get the warrants, and if he was just plain stupid."

Craig could only nod his agreement. He doubted Robins was that stupid.

"Is the Senator safely in Washington?" Bonnie asked, her voice low so only the four of them could hear the question.

"Safe and ready for a press conference right before he goes in for the vote tomorrow morning," Maxwell said, smiling. "All his close family and friends have been informed of the ruse so they won't worry."

"Even without being caught it seems that Robins is going to get his just desserts," Craig said. "I'd love to see his face as he watches that press conference."

All of them laughed and agreed.

Craig glanced at Hagar. "When are you going to want me in the station tomorrow morning?"

Hagar looked at his watch. "How about at the crack of noon?"

"Perfect," Craig said, feeling relieved that Hagar hadn't said eight. "Just over twelve hours of vacation."

"A good night's sleep," Bonnie said, sighing. "Won't that be a change for this trip?"

"Let me know what it feels like," Maxwell said.

"Yeah, me too," Hagar agreed.

Thirty minutes later Hagar dropped them off in front of the hotel and twenty minutes after that they were in their swimming suits and sitting in the bubbling water of the hotel's massive hot tub.

The tub was located in a corner of the swimming pool area. It was surrounded by boulders and made to look more like a natural hot springs than a hotel hot tub. Craig had to admit that was a nice touch. And the best part was that when sitting down in the tub, the boulders blocked the view of the pool and the hotel, leaving nothing but the rocky mountainside above the hotel and the night stars. It made for a wonderful relaxing hot dip in what felt like a mountain pool.

They were alone in the hot tub since it was almost one in the morning, but another couple was sitting on the far side of the pool, holding hands and talking while their feet dangled in the water.

"Perfect temperature," Bonnie said, letting her body float with the bubbles beside him. "A great meal and a hot soak. I think I needed this."

"I couldn't agree more," he said, leaning back and letting the warm water soothe his nerves. "Only one thing I need more than this and sleep."

She laughed. "And just what might that be?"

Without looking at her he said, "You have to ask?"

Her hand moved over and rested on his crotch. "What do you have in mind?"

"Maybe an hour of sex in that big bed upstairs," he said, "then eight hours of sleep, then another hour of sex tomorrow morning."

"Before or after breakfast?" she asked.

"On second thought," he said, "maybe both."

"Oh, feeling young, are we?"

"What are vacations for?"

She laughed as her hand moved slowly on him for a moment and he hardened under her touch.

Then she said, "That's a perfect plan if you add in just one thing."

"Trust me," he said, "the thing you're playing with is part of the plan."

She laughed again, but didn't stop moving her hand. "No, I just wanted to stay in the hot tub for a few more minutes. Let some of the tension drain away."

"Before we go back to the room and create more tension?" he asked.

"Exactly," she said.

Maybe, just maybe, they might be able to salvage this vacation after all.

CHAPTER TWENTY

Monday, April 10th
1:06 a.m.

CHARLES ROBINS SAT back in his chair and smiled as Grant reported the security measures being taken around the estate.

Charles figured that if he was going to have a problem with the man he called Bill because of the short payment, it was going to be tonight.

Or maybe tomorrow night.

So he had called in every member of his security team, under the leadership of Grant, an ex-Marine who knew more about defense and killing than Charles ever wanted to know.

He had told Grant who he needed kept out and Grant had said it would be no problem.

His people would keep everyone out.

Charles was just fine with that.

Grant had just finished explaining the basic defenses of the estate. He had two dozen men, all with state-of-the-art weapons patrolling both the grounds and the house. Three men watched the security monitors at all times, taking shifts. Automatic alarms had been set on every inch of the grounds' parameter. Grant was convinced that nothing was coming in that they didn't know about.

"Only one problem I see, Mr. Robins," Grant said.

"What's that?" Robins asked. The last thing he needed tonight was problems. So far everything had gone perfectly. Senator Knight wouldn't be voting later in the day and that was just about as perfect as it got.

"An FBI surveillance van is parked across the street from the main gate," Grant said without moving his hands from the parade rest position he had been standing in for five minutes, "and they have three other men stationed around the parameter of the estate in observation locations."

"FBI?" Robins asked, his stomach suddenly twisting in fear. "Are you sure?"

"Yes, sir," Grant said, "I'm sure. You pay me to be sure."

"Any idea why they are out there?" Robins asked.

"No, sir."

"Are they making any move to come in?" Robins asked.

Grant shook his head. "No, sir. They are strictly in surveillance mode."

Robins nodded. "So anyone coming in here would have to get past them as well as your people."

"No one will get past my people," Grant said. "But the FBI, in the configuration they are working out of, would make no move to stop anyone. The fight would be ours, sir."

Robins nodded. "Thank you, Grant. I will talk to you in the early morning."

"Have a good evening, sir," Grant said. He spun and moved briskly out of the study, the heels of his boots making no sound on the hardwood floor.

FBI? What were they doing out there?

He felt himself panic and he forced himself to take a few deep breaths, his palms flat on the hard wood of his desk top.

Clearly someone had put the vote tomorrow, and the implications to his companies' future, together with the Senator's accident. And since the FBI had failed in keeping the Senator from having his little spill down the hill, it would make sense they would cover all bases.

He forced himself to take more deep breaths and relax and think.

If anyone could prove anything, or even had a shred of evidence besides speculation, the FBI would have come in and taken him. So the fact that they were just in observation mode was good news as well.

That thought released his fear.

Of course. They had nothing on him but motive. And motive wasn't enough to move against someone like him, even if they did prove it wasn't an accident.

Charles stood and moved over to his bar and poured himself a small glass of his finest scotch. It was almost time to get some sleep. The legislation that would have killed his companies would not be passed. And by the time it could come up again, he would have enough votes controlled to stop it completely.

He had won.

He should learn to relax a little and savor the victories.

He downed the Scotch and moved toward the back entrance of his study that led up to his bedroom.

A few hours sleep was exactly what he needed.

CHAPTER TWENTY-ONE

Monday, April 10th
1:37 a.m.

BONNIE KNEW THAT even with Craig's plans of sex tonight and tomorrow morning—which she liked the sound of a lot—they were going to be lucky to stay awake long enough to make it happen. The last two days had been very stressful to both of them, and after the dip in the soothing warm water of the hot tub, Craig looked almost as tired as she felt.

Yet she wanted to make love to him as much as he said he wanted to make love to her. She could feel the desire slowly building, but she wasn't going to push it to happen tonight. They still had tomorrow and tomorrow night. More than enough time before heading home. She was just happy that they were out of the entire mess with the Senator.

She brushed her teeth and crawled into the wonderful-feeling clean sheets, letting them soothe her almost as much as the hot water had done earlier.

Craig had just finished brushing his teeth and was coming out of the bathroom naked when there was a knock on the door.

He glanced at her and she shrugged. One-thirty in the morning wasn't a normal time for anyone to come knocking.

"Who is it? Craig shouted at the door, moving at it to check through the peephole.

"Room service," Bonnie heard a man's voice on the other side respond.

Craig looked through the hole in the door, then said, "We didn't order any room service."

"Yes, I know, sir," Bonnie heard. "This is from a friend. A surprise."

Something was bothering her about that voice. About all this, but she couldn't put her finger on it.

Craig glanced back at Bonnie and just shook his head. Then he shouted through the door. "Hold on a second."

"Who would send us something at this time of the night?" Bonnie asked Craig as he climbed into a pair of shorts and padded back toward the door.

"I'm betting on Hagar," Craig said. "Or the Senator."

Bonnie nodded. That was possible. The Senator was a kind-enough man to do something like this all the way from Washington D.C..

But still, there was something wrong here.

Craig opened the door and stood back as a man in a hotel uniform pushed a food cart into the room.

"Hello," the man said to Bonnie as she held the sheets up under her chin.

Bonnie felt a shock run through her. She knew that voice from...

Suddenly, just as Craig was about to let the door close, two other men burst in, both pointing pistols at Craig.

"What the...?" Craig said, backing away from the door with his hands raised.

Before Bonnie could even react, the man in the hotel uniform pulled out a pistol and leveled it at her, motioning for her to remain still.

She pulled the sheet up even farther over her breasts and stared at the man.

The guy just smiled in return.

The door closed behind the three armed gunmen with a resounding thud

and Bonnie suddenly knew that she and Craig were far from out of this entire mess. In fact, they had just become part of the mess.

"I would suggest you both put some clothes on," the man in the hotel uniform said. "You're going for a ride to visit a friend." He smiled. "I told you it was a surprise."

Now Bonnie absolutely knew the voice. She would remember that voice anywhere. Standing in a hotel uniform with a gun pointed at her was the second man they had overheard on the golf course on Friday night.

She glanced at Craig, but he was staring at the two guns pointed at him.

"Let's go, people," the man said. "We honestly don't have all night."

Bonnie hadn't let another man see her nude since she married Craig, but at the moment it looked as if she didn't have much choice in the matter. She had no doubt this guy would shoot her without a second thought. And dying in this hotel room wasn't in her plans for the future.

She tossed the sheet aside and stood, moving over to where she had dropped her shorts and blouse when she had put on her swimming suit. With her back to the man, she dressed quickly.

By the time she turned around to again face the guns, Craig had on a golf shirt and was slipping on tennis shoes.

She retrieved her tennis shoes from near the bed and put them on as well.

When she stood, the man in the hotel uniform said, "Good. Now all three of us are going to walk down the hall and through the hotel lobby to a waiting limousine I have out front."

He pulled off the hotel uniform jacket and untucked his shirt to make himself look like a guest.

Craig glanced at Bonnie, but said nothing.

The man pointed his gun at Craig. "Detective, one false move in the hall or lobby and your pretty wife here will be the first to die, I promise you. My men and I have no problem firing in a public place. Chances are she will not be the only person to die. Am I understood?"

"Perfectly," Craig said.

"Good," the man said. He indicated they should go.

One of the gunmen opened the door and took up a position out in the hall, his gun inside a jacket pocket, but still very much in evidence.

Bonnie moved through the door beside Craig and walked beside him down the hall with the men following.

The ride down the elevator was long and uncomfortable, since Bonnie and Craig stood facing the door, the three men behind them. Bonnie could just imagine the three guns pointing at the small of her back. She didn't like the feeling at all.

The walk through the hotel lobby was just plain frightening. There had to be twenty people standing around or walking through the lobby. Couldn't they see what was happening?

It seemed that no one did.

There were no shouts or alarms and a few moments later they were out the front door, down the steps, and into the back of a waiting stretch limo.

The three men sat facing Bonnie and Craig. Two had their guns in their hands. The man clearly in charge just sat back and smiled.

Bonnie didn't feel like smiling back.

"Relax and enjoy the ride," the man said. "We don't have that far to go."

Neither Craig nor Bonnie said a word.

Bonnie had no idea why they were being taken and any question she might ask would only chance giving the man information he might not have. So she said nothing.

Outside the streets of Scottsdale flashed past, the night traffic very light on this early Monday morning.

CHAPTER TWENTY-TWO

Monday, April 10th
1:49 a.m.

CRAIG TRIED TO make sure he knew where they were, where they had turned, and what part of Scottsdale they were in. He wished he was more familiar with the area, but if needed, he might be able to retrace the steps from the hotel to the general area they were in now.

Maybe.

Their kidnappers sure seemed unconcerned that he was able to see where they were going. And that lack of concern bothered him. It usually meant that the kidnappers had no thoughts of ever letting them go.

The limo finally pulled over beside an open area, just short of a massive stone wall that towered twenty feet over the street and stretched for a least a half mile. Craig could see that there were a number of very large estates nearby, the biggest more than likely behind the wall. But right at this spot there was nothing but empty desert.

"Okay," the man said. "Time for a little talk."

He motioned for the two other gun-men to get out of the limo and then close the doors. When they did, he turned back to face Craig, smiling, his gun in his hand leveled on Bonnie's midsection.

"Just listen," the man said. "I have no desire to kill either of you. But make no mistake, I will if I have to."

Craig nodded and out of the corner of his eye he saw Bonnie do the same.

"First off, my name is not important. Charles Robins calls me Bill, so we'll just go with that."

Craig started at the name of Charles Robins. What was this guy up to anyway?

"I'll tell you this right up front," the man said, "Charles Robins hired me to stage an accident with Senator Knight so that Knight would not be able to vote later today in Washington on a piece of legislation that would hurt Robins."

Craig desperately wanted to tell this guy that he had failed, but knew that wouldn't be a good idea at this point. The guy would find out soon enough as it was.

The bigger question is why this guy was telling them all this information?

"I have put tapes of my conversations with Mr. Robins in a locker at the train station." The man flipped Bonnie the key.

She was so surprised that she almost didn't catch it.

"The locker number is on the key. If you get out of this alive, that's the key to the locker."

Craig, in all his years of police work, had never been this confused before. "So why are you telling us this?" Craig asked.

The guy laughed. "I suppose this all does seem a little odd to a police detec-tive used to criminals trying to cover their guilt instead of admit it."

"A little," Craig said, as sarcastically as he could.

The man snickered. "Trust me, Detective, I will never be caught for this crime."

Now Craig understood. "But you want Charles Robins to be, is that it?"

"Exactly," the man said.

"Why?" Bonnie asked.

"Because the man wouldn't pay me what we agreed he should pay me for the work I did."

Now it was Craig's turn to laugh. "The old saying comes back to bite you, huh?"

The guy smiled at Craig. "You are right, detective. No honor among thieves is how the saying goes. But I keep my word and I expect others to do the same. Charles Robins did not."

"And now he must pay the price," Bonnie said. "Is that it?"

"Exactly," the man said.

"So couldn't you have just called the police, left the tape, and ran like hell," Craig asked. "Why go through all the problems of kidnapping us?"

"For one I would have never had the pleasure of seeing your fine wife here without clothes on."

Beside him Craig could feel Bonnie tighten even more, but she said nothing and didn't move.

"Secondly," the man said, going on, "Charles Robins is an idiot and I want to make sure he is so deep into this mess that no amount of money will buy his way out."

"And that's where we come in," Craig said. "Right?"

"Exactly," the man said. "Let's go."

With that he opened the door, and with the point of his gun, indicated that they should get out of the limo.

Craig climbed out with Bonnie behind him, followed by the man.

Outside a third man had joined the other two. He was very large and mus-cled, with a military posture and build. He was perfectly proportioned and as Craig got closer he realized the guy had to be at least six-four.

The big man nodded to the one who had been talking to them in the limo, then turned to the other two guards. "Tie their hands behind their backs."

Each guard did as he was told.

Craig could feel the rope being pulled painfully tight as he attempted to keep his wrists apart and his muscles flexed.

"Ow!" Bonnie said, glancing back at the guy behind her. "Not so damned tight. I might need those hands again."

After they were finished being tied, the tall man turned to the guards. "Take our two prisoners to Mr. Robins' study, then have him awakened. Give him this note."

The big man handed the guard behind Craig a piece of paper.

"Through the front gate, sir?" the guard asked.

"Does it matter to you?" the large man demanded, moving up into the guard's face. "Or would you like me to do it and find someone to take your place?"

The big man towered over both Craig and the guard.

Craig could hear the guard swallow behind him.

"No, sir," the guard said, clearly afraid of the big man.

Smart thinking.

Craig wouldn't want to tangle with the guy either.

"Now follow orders," the big man said. "I have another task to complete."

The guard pushed Craig down the street while the other shoved Bonnie ahead of him.

After about twenty steps Craig glanced back over his shoulder. The man they had overheard on the fairway on Friday, the man who had told them he was hired to complete the plot against the Senator, was climbing back into the limo with the larger man. Both were laughing.

That made Craig shiver.

Craig looked ahead at the distant front gate to what must be Charles Robins' walled estate. And just to the right, sitting peacefully on the street, was the white van Craig knew held the FBI observers. Maxwell was going to go nuts when he saw this on tape.

If Craig had had his hands free, he would have waved as they passed.

And that was exactly what the guy who had kidnapped them had wanted.

He and Bonnie were bait.

The FBI was the weapon.

And the target was Charles Robins.

Craig had a feeling that getting him and Bonnie out of this alive was going to take more luck than he wanted to admit.

CHAPTER TWENTY-THREE

Monday, April 10th
2:17 a.m.

CHARLES ROBINS DIDN'T much like getting awakened in the middle of his sleep. And tonight was no exception.

Yet the guard didn't seem to want to let it go.

"I'm sorry, sir," the guard said, his voice seeming to blare over the private intercom. "It is important that you come to your study at once."

"I'll be right there," Robins said. He crawled out of bed slowly, rubbing his face. Screw going right there. He was in charge here, and he'd get down there in his own damned time.

It took him ten minutes to put on clothes, use the bathroom, and pour himself a glass of juice before he finally went down the private stairs to his office.

He expected Grant to be there with some problem, standing at attention in front of his desk like he always did. But instead he saw two guards with a tied-up man and woman. Both the man and the woman were in shorts.

"What's this all about?" he demanded.

"Charles Robins, I presume," the tied man said.

"And just who the hell are you?" Robins asked.

"I'm Detective Frakes," the guy said, smiling. He nodded at the woman beside him. "This is Officer Stanley. We're both with the Seattle police department."

Robins felt his stomach clamp up into a tight ball. These were the two who had been playing with Senator Knight all weekend. What in the hell were they doing here?

"What were you two trying to do, break in to my estate?"

The man shook his head no. "I'm afraid your men came and got us from our hotel room bed."

Charles glared at the guard. "Is that true?"

"Yes, sir," the guard said.

Charles just stared at the guard, not really believing what he had been told. His men had kidnapped two cops, the same two who had been playing for two days with Senator Knight, from their hotel room and brought them to his study.

"Why would you do that?" Charles almost screamed. "Where's Grant?"

Charles stared at one guard, then the other.

The guard behind the tied-up detective stepped forward. "Grant told me to give you this note, sir,"

"Note?" Charles asked. "I don't want any note. I want to talk to him. Now!"

The guard only shook and looked afraid, so Robins took the note and opened it.

Dear Charles,

Since you saw fit to short me one-half-million dollars for the job you hired me to do on Senator Knight, I felt you deserved something for my troubles.

Enjoy,
Bill

Underneath the first note there was a second hand-scrawled note in another color pen. It said:

Dear Mr. Robins,

I cannot work for a man who would hurt a Senator and kidnap fellow police officers. I quit.

Sincerely,
Grant

"Damn, damn, damn," Charles said, reading the notes over again. There was no chance at all of being able to show this note to anyone. He stopped and looked up at the guard. "You said Grant gave you this note?"

"Yes, sir," the guard said.

"Was there another man with Grant when he gave it to you?"

"Yes, sir," the guard said. "A man who called himself Bill."

Suddenly the past few years were all making sense. It was no wonder this Bill

125

person could get into the estate through the security so easily every time he was called. He and Grant, his chief of security, had been working together all this time.

And now the guy had made Charles look as if he had ordered the kidnapping of these two police officers. And that might be enough to tie him to what happened to Senator Knight. With the motive, it was more than enough, that was for sure.

Charles moved over and sat down behind his desk, trying to clear his mind.

He had to figure out what to do next.

And no option looked good.

"Sir?" the guard asked, "what do I do with the prisoners?"

Charles glanced at the two cops, then shook his head. "Put them in a closet and guard them until I decide what to do next."

"But sir," the guard said, "the FBI knows they are in here."

"Of course they do," Charles said. "Don't you think I know that? Now do as I say. And for god's sake, don't hurt them."

As the two were being led out Charles drank his juice as calmly as he could. He hadn't thought of the FBI. The man named Bill had set a perfect trap.

Charles leaned back and looked around at his beautiful study. With the Senator not voting tomorrow, he was going to keep control of his fortune. And that meant he could afford the expensive attorneys who could get him off this hook.

He would blame Grant and the man named Bill as getting greedy, as taking too much control in his problems. His lawyers would get him off as a man who let his employees take too much control.

He could feel the plan starting to form. In a few hours he would turn over

the two detectives personally, claiming he just had learned about the plan.

If he worked it right, with enough spin and good enough attorneys, he might just come out of this all right.

CHAPTER TWENTY-FOUR

Monday, April 10th
2:36 a.m.

THE GUARDS SHOVED them both into a small hall closet and closed the door, plunging them into darkness.

Bonnie bumped against Craig and then used the right wall of the closet to get her balance. The ropes around her wrists had become painful about ten minutes after they had been put on, and now they were just a dull ache. From what she saw before they were shoved inside, the closet had a few coats hanging in it, all on wooden hangers. Nothing more.

"You all right?" Craig whispered.

"Fine," she whispered back, keeping her voice soft enough so that no one outside the closet could hear. "Just completely confused."

She still couldn't believe what had happened to them.

Taken from their hotel room by a man who wanted to frame another man. Then told about it.

It was just too weird.

"Seems like we're pawns in a game between murderers," Craig said, his voice low and coming out of the darkness. "I sure don't much like that idea."

"I couldn't agree more," she said. "That Charles Robins gives me the creeps."

"Slime describes him just fine," Craig said.

"So what do you think is going to happen next?" Bonnie asked. "You think the FBI guys saw us?"

"They would have had to be asleep to miss us," Craig said.

"It's getting lighter in here," Bonnie said.

Her eyes were adjusting to the dim light coming through under the door and around the cracks in the casing. She could barely see the outline of Craig leaning against the other wall a foot or so from her.

"It is," Craig said. "And we have to be ready for anything that's going to happen next. How tight are your ropes?"

"Tight," she said. "But I can still move my fingers."

"So can I," he said. "You want to try untying mine first?"

"Sure," she said, turning her back to him. "Let me get into a stable position and you put your ropes in my hands."

"Good idea," he said.

Bonnie leaned forward, head against the wall for balance. Behind her she could feel Craig's hands against hers. Then he lowered his hands so that her fingers were on the ropes around his wrists.

The knots felt tight and it took her a moment to find a place to even try to start working the knot loose.

Then she noticed that Craig's fingers were between her legs, against her crotch because of how she was leaning forward.

She moved her butt slightly. "This could be more fun than I thought."

He laughed lightly and moved his fingers against the seam of her shorts, keeping his wrists still so she could work on the knot.

She could feel that she was making a little progress, but not much. "Can you move your wrists to your right slightly, and turn them to the left?"

"Sure," he said. As he moved to the right he slipped one finger under the leg of her shorts and pulled up as he twisted his wrists to the left.

That put two of his fingers right up against her bare flesh. She made herself focus on untying the knot.

"No underwear," he whispered. "Nice."

His fingers moved back and forth.

She tried to focus on the knot, and it seemed to be coming free slowly, but Craig's fingers were distracting her.

"That feels wonderful," she said softly. "But you're not helping me get you untied."

His fingers stopped. She desperately wanted to push back against them, but the fear of losing the progress she made on the knot stopped her.

She forced herself to work at the rope, ignoring the sense of his touch against her crotch.

What seemed like an eternity later she said, "I think I've almost got it."

His fingers slid a little farther along her crotch.

"I'd agree with that," he said, the humor clear in his voice even in the dark.

"You keep that up and I'm never going to get this untied," she said.

"Nothing but promises," he said, laughing as his fingers moved a little again and then stopped. The movement sent chills through her, and small ripples of pleasure swirling in her stomach.

She focused on the knot, finally pulling it free.

"Got it," she said.

"Nice job," he said. "Stay put and I'll untie you."

She could feel his hands working on the ropes on her wrists, and as he did she moved her butt back against his crotch.

"Now you're the one slowing down this process," he said.

"Well then hurry up and get me untied," she said, moving her butt slowly back and forth. She loved teasing him, just as he loved teasing her.

Finally she felt the wonderful relief of the ropes coming off. She stood up and rubbed her wrists, trying to get circulation back through them. She had no doubt she was going to have bruises there for weeks.

"Now what?" she asked.

Craig kissed her quickly, then turned and pulled one of the wooden hangers off the bar. He slapped it against his hand. "Get one and let's see if we can get out of here."

She did as he suggested, the weight of the hanger in her hands not giving her any reassurance at all.

Craig turned and carefully tried the door handle. It was locked and as he tried to turn it, the knob rattled.

"You two stay quiet in there," a guards voice came from the other side of the door, loud and very, very close. "You'll be let out soon enough."

"Shit," Craig whispered.

Bonnie turned and put the hanger back on the hook, then sat down on the floor, her back against the back wall of the closet. They weren't getting out of this closet any time soon.

She watched as Craig gave the closet one more close inspection and then sat down beside her.

"What a way to spend a vacation," she whispered.

"As long as it's with you," Craig said, "I'd spend it locked in a closet."

"We are locked in a closet," she said.

"Oh," was all he said.

CHAPTER TWENTY-FIVE

Monday, April 10th
3:10 a.m.

MAXWELL LOOKED AT the rumpled and very tired Hagar as he staggered into the police station. A couple other night-shift detectives laughed, but no one said anything.

"This had better be damned good," Hagar said. "I was dreaming about swimming naked with a dozen women when you so rudely woke me up."

Maxwell laughed. "No wonder you look so tired." He pointed at the screen of a monitor sitting on a desk and punched play. He had watched these images a dozen times over the last ten minutes and still couldn't figure out exactly what they meant.

Hagar frowned. The image showed a tall wall and some people coming down the street toward the camera.

"The Robins estate," Maxwell said. "Filmed less than an hour ago."

"I know where it's at," Hagar said, "but who are the people?"

"Wait," Maxwell said.

On screen the images of the people became clearer and clearer.

"Holy shit, you're kidding?"

"I'm not," Maxwell said. "That's Bonnie and Craig, their hands tied, being led into the

Robins estate by two of Robins' goons. I checked their room and they are not there."

"Robins kidnapped them?" Hagar almost shouted as the film showed Bonnie and Craig being walked right through the front gate. "Why the hell would he do that?"

"I don't know the answer to that question," Maxwell said, "but they haven't come out of there yet."

Hagar shook his head. "Didn't they know your van was there filming everything?"

"I guess not," Maxwell said. "Or I doubt they would have taken them in this way."

Hagar glanced at Maxwell. "Are you thinking what I think you are thinking? You want to go in after them?"

Maxwell nodded. "I've got agents flying up here from Tucson and down from Vegas. I can have a force of over thirty men ready to roll in forty minutes."

"And you think Bonnie and Craig are still alive in there?" Hagar asked.

"At the moment I do," Maxwell said, "but the longer we wait, the less chance I give them. And I give them no chance when Robins discovers they helped trick him with the Senator."

"Damn, you're right," Hagar said. He rewound the film again quickly and watched them walk past the truck and through the main gate.

To Maxwell there was no doubt both Craig and Bonnie were tied and being led at gunpoint.

"Robins might have over fifty men in there," Hagar said, "and from what I've observed about those men, they aren't afraid to defend that place."

"I assumed as much," Maxwell said. "That's why we need to work together on this."

Hagar just stared at him for a moment, then said, "You're nuts, you know that?"

Maxwell nodded.

"Shit, shit, shit!" Hagar said, turning from Maxwell and picking up the phone.

Ten minutes later Hagar had permission to work with the FBI from the Chief of Police.

Thirty minutes later Hagar had a force of over fifty men, including a SWAT team from Phoenix, staged at different locations around the Robins estate, armed and ready to go when the order was given.

Maxwell knew that if this turned into a gunfight, it was going to go down poorly. Their best bet was to try to talk their way in and disarm guards as they went.

Hagar was convinced that there was going to be no talking their way inside those walls. He had calls out for even more help to stand ready. He told Maxwell that if this didn't turn out to be the Alamo west, he'd be surprised.

That was the last thing Maxwell wanted to have happen. But inside those walls were two kidnapped cops and a man they suspected of trying to kill a United States Senator. He had no other choice.

They had to go in.

CHAPTER TWENTY-SIX

Monday, April 10th
4:03 a.m.

BONNIE HAD DOZED lightly for most of the past half hour, and Craig had let her. The closet had gotten cold and Bonnie had pulled down one of the expensive wool coats that hung in there to use as a cover. And she was using Craig as a pillow, something he didn't mind at all.

Craig had talked her into closing her eyes for a short time. There was just no point in both of them trying to stay alert. There wasn't much they could do until Robins decided to let them out. Unless they wanted to take a chance on getting shot trying to escape, and at the moment Craig didn't much like that idea.

So until something happened, they sat on the floor, in the dark, and waited.

Craig guessed that at least an hour or more had gone by since Robins had tossed them into the closet. And if that was the case, they were getting closer and closer to the Senator's press conference in Washington. Craig had no desire to still be Robins' prisoner when he discovered the Senator was still healthy and voting.

A slight snoring noise rumbled the closet and Craig eased Bonnie sideways. Usually she didn't snore, but considering how tired she was, and the circumstances, it was understandable.

Bonnie mumbled and cuddled against his side as the snoring sound happened again. He shook her lightly, then when her eyes popped open he whispered, "Shhh, listen."

The snoring sound came again.

She sat upright in the darkness, then leaned toward him and whispered, "The guard's asleep."

"That's what I thought," Craig said.

"Think we can break that lock open?" she asked, her voice barely audible.

"Yeah," he said, silently standing and moving his legs to make sure the circulation hadn't left them. He had taken out other locks much stronger than the one on this closet door. And from the sounds of

the snoring, the guard was leaning against the door. So the break-out would have to be strong enough to snap the lock and shove the guard aside at the same time. If the wood in the door held, it would work.

"What do you want me to do?" Bonnie asked.

"Be ready to hit the guy on the head with one of those wooden hangers," Craig whispered.

The snoring stopped for an instant, the guy shifted against the door, moving more away from the lock, then a moment later the snoring started again.

Craig let out the breath he had been holding. "Ready?"

"As I'll ever be," Bonnie whispered.

Craig braced himself against the back wall of the closet. It was just a little too far from the door to give him the best force on his kick. He used both hands to lightly pull on the hanger bar. It seemed very solid and secure in place. It would hold his weight long enough for him to kick the door open, he was sure.

He leaned toward Bonnie and whispered, "Here we go."

"Careful," she whispered back.

"You too," he said.

He put himself in position directly behind the door's handle, then with two deep breaths, he pulled himself up on the bar and with all the force he could manage in both legs, kicked the door with both feet.

It smashed open like it hadn't even been latched.

Bonnie was through the door before he could even let go of the bar.

The guard had been shoved head over heels away from the door by the force of Craig's kicks.

Bonnie was around the open door and over the guard by the time the guy even started to get up. One very hard smack against the side of the head with the wooden hanger and the guy went back to sleep.

"He's going to have one massive headache when he wakes up," Bonnie said, smiling at her husband.

"Remind me to never get you mad at me."

Craig grabbed the guy's rifle, a semi-automatic with a dozen rounds in the clip. The guy had one in the chamber, ready to fire.

Bonnie dug around in the guard's pockets and pulled out two more clips for the rifle and a 44 caliber pistol with extra rounds. Then she took an earplug from the guard's ear and a small communications device from his front pocket of his vest.

She handed the communication equipment to Craig.

"Better find out what his name is," Craig said, "so we can answer a call to him."

Bonnie quickly flipped the guy over and dug his wallet out of his back pocket. She flipped it open and then snorted. "Dwight. His name is Dwight."

A security guard named Dwight. No wonder he had fallen asleep.

She stuck the wallet back in the guy's pants and stood.

"Keep watch," he said.

He grabbed the guard and pulled him back into the closet, then tied his hands and feet with the rope they had been tied with.

The closet door, with a little work, almost looked like nothing had happened to it by the time Craig got it closed again.

"Now what?" Bonnie asked.

Craig glanced down the corridor. There was a security camera trained on

the corner about fifty feet away. And another one in the other direction down the hall. It looked like they were between them at least.

"There's got to be a major security system in this place, as well as at least twenty guards, if not a lot more," he said. He pointed at the cameras as he stuck the earplug in his ear.

"Damn," she said, "we move from here at all and they'll know we've escaped."

"So when we do move, we make the best of it," Craig said, "and move fast."

"Until then we wait here?" Bonnie asked.

In his ear Craig could hear the sudden excited talking of the front guards, as well as others along the perimeter of the estate. They were all reporting in that a large number of police had suddenly moved up into position.

"Exactly," he said, smiling at her. "But I don't think we're going to have to wait long. We're about to have the cavalry come to the rescue."

CHAPTER TWENTY-SEVEN

Monday, April 10th
4:27 a.m.

"ARE WE READY?" Maxwell asked Hagar.

"My people are," Hagar said, nodding as he listened to the last of status reports in his ear.

"So are mine," Maxwell said. "Let's do it."

Maxwell picked up a bullhorn as the two of them stepped around the police car and walked ten feet out into the middle of the road in front of the main gate of the Robins estate. Above them the stars were shining and the air was crisp and almost cold. Maxwell could see a dozen men in different positions inside the gate, guns all at rest. As long as they stayed that way, everything would be fine.

"Attention. This is the FBI," Maxwell shouted through the bullhorn, his voice echoing over the estate and into the rock hills behind it. "Open the gates and throw down your weapons. You are completely surrounded."

Nothing.

He knew that he had the horn set loud enough that anyone inside the buildings beyond those wall would be able to hear him as well. He would give good old Robins a moment to think about things, and then try again.

The silence of the late desert night seemed intense as Maxwell and Hagar waited. Inside the gate no one moved.

"This is the FBI!" Maxwell repeated through the horn. "Throw down your weapons and come out."

Again the silence seemed to crawl down over him like a giant bug trying to smother him. He could feel his own heart beating and the fear choking him. But he stood there, in the middle of the road, and waited for a response.

Then through the gate there was movement, but it took Maxwell a fraction of a second to realize it was the wrong kind of movement. One of the men just inside the gate to the right was raising his gun.

Another behind him was doing the same.

"Get down!" Hagar shouted and turned to get to cover.

Maxwell spun and ran, the ten steps between him and the shelter of the patrol car seemingly a thousand yards.

The air suddenly echoed with the sounds of gunfire. For an instant it was only a few shots, all coming from beyond the walls, then there was more and more until it was impossible to tell how many, as if strings of firecrackers were being shot off in a closed space.

Maxwell's agents were now returning fire, trying to cover him as he and Hagar got to shelter.

A bullet smashed into the car just beyond him.

Close!

Way too damned close!

He tried to dive for the shelter of the front fender of the car.

He didn't make it.

The burning feeling of the bullet cutting through the flesh of his back wasn't as bad as he expected. But the impact flipped him completely over, smashing him to the concrete. The fall hurt like hell, and he banged his head, knocking him into blackness for a moment.

He came to in time to feel Hagar's hands grab him and drag him beyond the car and over into a shallow ditch beside the road.

There was no pain.

That surprised him.

He just couldn't move.

That also surprised him.

He should feel pain, he should be able to move. It was as if the wind had been knocked out of him and all his energy taken.

"Damn!" Hagar said. "Officer down here!"

Two other men swarmed into the ditch beside him as the gun battle continued, the quiet of the night now a continuous roar of explosions.

Maxwell noted it all like watching it from a distance. For some reason he knew that things were not going well, but a part of him just no longer cared.

"Hang in there," Hagar yelled to him, but it was like the cop was shouting down a long tunnel.

Maxwell felt himself smile.

He had been shot and it hadn't really hurt.

And now he was going to die. He knew that as clearly as he had known anything in his life.

And that was all right as well.

This experience was not at all what he had expected death to feel like.

He looked up at the pained expression on Hagar's face and knew exactly what the cop wanted him to say.

How he knew, he wasn't sure, but he just knew.

He used one hand to pull Hagar down closer, then in his ear he said, "Get the damned son-of-a-bitch for me, would you?"

"I will," Hagar said.

Maxwell really didn't care, but he knew that Hagar did. And if the situation was reversed, Hagar would have said it for him as well.

Maxwell felt he was floating now, sort of watching what was happening to him like an observer from a distance. He was both in his body and watching them around his body.

There was no pain.

Just a wonderful sense of floating.

"Maxwell!"

The voice sort of pulled at him, but he ignored it. He liked the floating.

"Maxwell!" Hagar shouted. "Maxwell, stay with us!"

But Maxwell could see no point in staying.

And with that he died.

CHAPTER TWENTY-EIGHT

Monday, April 10th
4:32 a.m.

CRAIG WAS STUNNED when the shooting began.

"What the hell is going on?" Bonnie asked, clearly as afraid and as stunned as he was. They had both heard the faint demands of Maxwell as he told Robins' men to lay down their guns and come out. At the time the voice had cheered them.

Then in his ear Craig had heard the command come from Robins directly. "Keep the FBI out at all costs."

A moment later the shooting had started.

"The stupid ass ordered them to fight the FBI," Craig said, shaking his head in amazement. "What the hell is he thinking?"

"Maybe that's our problem," Bonnie said. "We keep expecting the man to think."

"Well, we need to stop this," Craig said. "There's a lot of good men out there getting fired on."

"And just two of us in here," Bonnie said. "You got any smart ideas?"

"Sure," Craig said. "We capture the head of this snake and tell him to shut things down."

Bonnie nodded and glanced down the hall. "I can remember how to get back to his study, but we're going to have to do it fast and without stopping."

"Agreed," Craig said. "I'll take the lead and you cover my back."

She pinched his butt. "I'll make sure this doesn't get shot off if you take care of that guy in front."

"Deal," he said.

Outside the gunfire was becoming even more intense. It was a war out there and unless it stopped quickly a lot of people were going to get hurt or killed.

He kissed her and then turned and headed down the hall, knowing she was right behind him.

At that moment what he really wanted was to lock them both in a closet and only come out when the shooting was over, but he knew neither one of them could do that.

They were cops. It was their lives.

And right now a lot of other cops were getting shot at. If they had the best chance of stopping it, they needed to take it.

They had to take it.

With the rifle leveled and ready to fire he went around the first corner under the camera. There was no one in the hallway.

He kept moving at a near run.

Bonnie stayed close behind, the sound of her footsteps almost matching his.

In about fifty paces the hallway opened up into a wide foyer with plants on one side and a door leading outside to the right.

The door into Robins' study was to the left and down another short hallway.

There was a guard poised, facing the exterior door, as if waiting for someone to come through.

Craig shouted, "Drop the gun!"

The guard was too stupid for words.

Instead of dropping the gun he spun and tried to fire.

Craig cut him down with a short blast, almost ripping the guard in half with the tight pattern of his bullets.

"To the left!" Bonnie said behind him and Craig headed that way.

Ahead of him a guard poked his head out of a door and Craig fired through the edge of the door and wood of the wall, aiming at where the man's midsection would be.

The guy jerked and fell out into the hallway, clearly dead. Any good cop knew that the wood and plasterboard of regular house walls didn't stop most bullets. This guy clearly had watched too much television thinking he was safe behind that door.

"Grab his rifle," Craig said as he checked the room the guard had been in for anyone else, and then moved on down the hall.

Robins' study was two more doors away.

Bonnie grabbed the rifle and kept guard behind him as Craig stared at that office door.

There was no doubt that there was someone on the other side of it waiting for him to come through.

And the minute he did, he was dead.

He didn't want to be dead just yet.

But there was a guy here that already had that distinction, and wouldn't mind a few more holes, Craig figured.

Craig went back and picked up the guy he had just killed, keeping the rifle in one hand as he did it. The dead guy wasn't that heavy, or the adrenaline in Craig's body was working overtime.

The guy's blood got on his hands, but Craig ignored it.

"Get on the floor and cover me," he said to his wife and rushed at the study door, the guy's body a shield ahead of him.

Just before he reached the door he tossed the body as hard as he could, using his running momentum to get the body to hit the door halfway up and at a good speed.

Then Craig dropped to the carpet, rifle pointed ahead.

The body smashed open the study door and was instantly peppered with bullets, making the dead man jerk and flip his arms as he dropped.

Now Available
from all your favorite booksellers in trade paper and electronic editions.

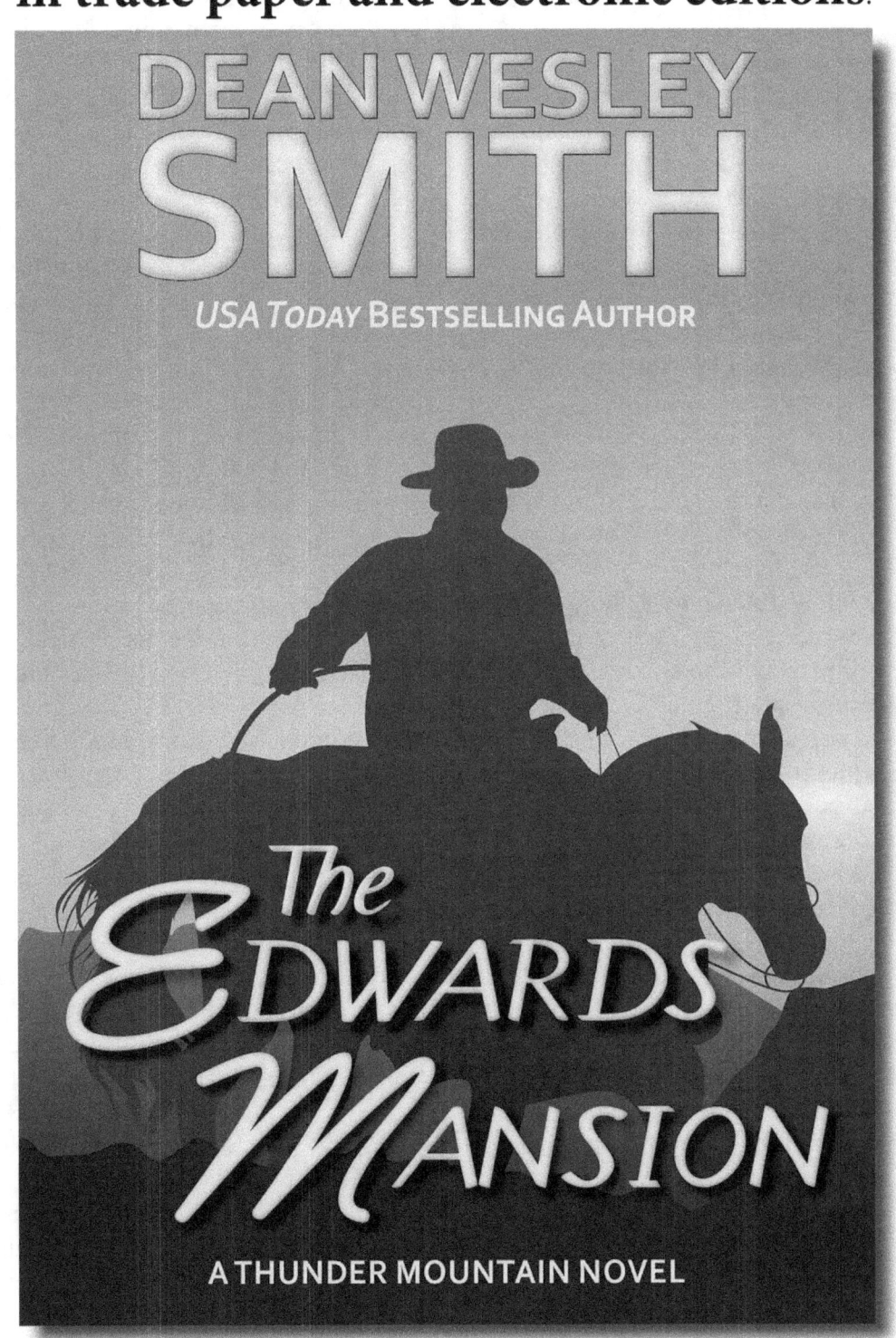

DEAN WESLEY SMITH

USA Today BESTSELLING AUTHOR

The EDWARDS MANSION

A THUNDER MOUNTAIN NOVEL

Craig had his gun up and firing before the body was out of the way.

Almost instantly the gunfire from inside the study stopped. A moment later there was the sound of a gun hitting the floor.

Craig dove over the dead man and rolled, coming up with his rifle facing Charles Robins' scared face and his shaking hand that was holding a small pistol.

To Robins' right was the guard who had been firing, now slumped in, and bleeding all over, an expensive leather chair.

"I would suggest you drop that gun now," Bonnie said, moving to cover her husband. "I would love to pull this trigger and blow those tiny brains of yours all over your desk."

Charles glanced at her, then dropped his gun like it was suddenly too hot to hold.

Craig used the barrel of his rifle to kick the gun onto the floor.

"Now," he said to Robins, "tell your men to drop their weapons and surrender."

Robins hesitated until Craig raised his rifle and pointed it at the man's head. Then Robins picked up a small communications unit and said, "Attention. This is Robins. Drop your weapons now. Cease fire."

Slowly the noise of gunfire died off, replaced by a wonderful silence filled only by distant sirens.

"Tell them to put their hands on their heads and walk toward the nearest cop until told otherwise," Craig said.

Robins hesitated.

"Oh, please let me shoot him," Bonnie said, moving up and putting her gun against the side of his head.

"Oh, I kind of like this side of you," Craig said, smiling at her.

"Let me pull the trigger and see how hot it gets me," she said, winking at him.

Robins instantly moved to do as Craig had ordered, repeating his words exactly. He clearly believed Bonnie would kill him.

"Now what?" Robins asked as he finished.

"Now we shoot you," Bonnie said, raising her gun again.

"She's just kidding," Craig said, smiling at the sick look on Robins' face. "But I won't hesitate. So come on out from behind there and sit at the feet of your dead man there."

Robins did as Craig told him until he stood over his dead guard. Then he turned and shook his head. "I can't do that."

"You caused his death," Craig said. "Seems you owe him a little company. Now sit down."

Craig jammed his rifle into Robins' chest and the man dropped to the floor.

Craig took the dead man's arms and placed them around Robins' neck, as if the man was giving his boss a hug from behind. Blood dripped down the front of Robins' shirt from the man's hand.

"Now isn't that sweet?" Bonnie asked Craig.

Craig couldn't think of a better thing to have happen to the man who wanted Senator Knight dead. And who had ordered his men to fire on police.

Charles Robins looked as if he might throw up at any minute, but with Bonnie's rifle leveled on his chest, he didn't move.

Ten minutes later Hagar and a dozen others swarmed into the room. Once they saw that Craig and Bonnie had it under control, they stopped and all but two of them moved off to finish checking the house.

"I was wondering why they suddenly stopped firing and gave up," Hagar said.

Craig pointed at where Robins still sat with the dead guard's arms around his neck. "He just needed a little convincing is all. And Bonnie is a real good convincer."

Craig smiled at his wife as she nodded her thanks.

"Does he know about Senator Knight's press conference yet?" Hagar asked.

"When is that scheduled?" Bonnie asked, smiling at the startled look from Robins.

"Eight eastern time," Hagar said. "Just about any moment now."

"Well," Craig said, "Bonnie turn it on while someone reads Mr. Robins his rights."

Hagar got down on one knee in front of Robins, and without moving the dead man's arms off the guy's shoulders, read Charles Robins his rights.

A moment later, on CNN, the serious face of Senator Knight appeared and began to talk.

For a short moment Charles Robins just stared at the screen, then slowly he closed his eyes.

"Ain't justice wonderful?" Craig asked, listening as Senator Knight thanked him and Bonnie for saving his life.

CHAPTER TWENTY-NINE

Monday, April 10th
6:36 a.m.

THE LIMO PULLED through the gate and out onto the tarmac of the Scottsdale airport, stopping beside the two private jets just as the sun was breaking over the hills to the east. A moment later the man Charles Robins called Bill finished his last phone call. He hung up the phone, then flipped closed the laptop computer he had been holding on his lap.

"Well?" Grant asked.

Bill looked across the private area of the limo at his old friend Grant and smiled.

"Done?" Grant asked.

"Done," Bill said. "We've just moved over sixty-seven million of Charles Robins' company's money to varied accounts, and then on to other numbered accounts. It will be moved automatically another hundred times, in varied amounts, before it finally settles in our accounts."

"As always no one can trace it?" Grant asked.

"Trust me," Bill said, "if someone does try to trace it, it will look like Charles did it himself. And the money will be gone. Hell, it will take a team of auditors years to find everything that's missing."

Grant laughed, the sound filling the limo. "The man was just too stupid for words."

"That he was. And I must say, it was a pleasure taking him for every penny."

"It almost makes taking orders from the idiot for four years worth it."

"Sixty-seven million?" Bill said, laughing. "I'd say that was worth it. You got us access to everything the man owned, every password, every account. And the guy let you." Bill shook his head at the craziness of it all.

Grant laughed, his big frame shaking. "Sure hope those two nice cops from Seattle got out of that firefight alive. She was a looker."

"I'm sure they did," Bill said. "They were smart enough to save the Senator, they're smart enough to get out of Robins' house, I'm sure."

"I sure wanted to tell old Robins about Senator Knight being just fine in Washington, D.C.," Grant said, laughing.

"If he doesn't know by now," Bill said, "he will shortly."

The two men laughed again and climbed out of the limo.

Bill looked at the two planes. One jet waited for him, the other for Grant. They were headed in two different directions.

In a matter of hours they would both be far out of the reach of Charles Robins and the FBI. In a matter of days they would both have new identities and enough money to last a very long time.

"Well, friend," Grant said, shaking his hand. "When will I see you again?"

"Oh, a year or so. As soon as I find another sucker like Robins. I'll be in touch."

"Take your time," Grant said. "I think I've got enough to last for a few years."

The man who had been called Bill laughed.

They let go of the handshake and turned for their jets.

It was the third time they had done this to a stupid, greedy businessman like Robins. They both knew it wouldn't be the last. They enjoyed the score too much. It made life worth living for both of them.

Bill's jet left the runway first, followed a minute later by Grant's.

In the air one jet turned west, the other south.

EPILOGUE

Friday, April 14th
10:12 p.m.

MONDAY HAD TURNED into a day from hell for both of them. Bonnie could not remember a day like it before. They had had no sleep and millions of questions to answer, forms to fill out, details to go over.

And all while trying to understand that Maxwell had been killed.

Bonnie found his death almost impossible to believe for some reason. The guy seemed like he always had everything under control. But clearly he had made one mistake, and that was walking into the line of fire of that estate's front gate.

Hagar had told them that he was lucky to get back when the firing started.

Bonnie still hadn't believed Maxwell was dead until the funeral on Thursday. Then finally she had allowed herself to cry for the man she had only known a short time.

By six in the evening on Monday they had been allowed to return to their hotel room for a shower and change of clothes.

But Hagar had had a car bring them right back to the station.

By midnight Monday they had finished almost everything that needed to be done immediately, and were allowed to go back to the hotel to sleep.

By eight the next morning they were back at the station.

The hearings and interviews seemed to stretch forever. Over and over again, both together and separately, Bonnie and

Craig had answered questions about what had happened the entire weekend.

All day Tuesday, all day Wednesday, after Maxwell's funeral on Thursday, and then even more questions on Friday morning.

Finally, Friday afternoon they had been set free. Bonnie had felt numb and more tired than she had felt in years.

On Wednesday, Charles Robins had been arraigned on more counts than Bonnie believed was possible to charge one man with. And fifty-six of his men were under charges of attempted murder, murder, and so on. Besides Maxwell, ten others had died, all Robins' men. Ten cops and two FBI agents had been wounded, but only one seriously.

The firefight, combined with Senator Knight's sudden appearance in Washington, made all the national news and created a massive media stir around the police headquarters in Scottsdale that didn't die off until Thursday.

Somewhere in the middle of Monday afternoon, Bonnie remembered talking to her boss in Seattle, telling her they wouldn't be back for at least a week. Her boss completely understood.

Now it was Friday again. One week after they had first arrived for a weekend golf tournament. They had both taken naps in the afternoon and got out on the putting green and practiced for a few hours after dinner. But neither of their hearts were into playing golf.

As it was getting dark, Craig had suggested they go for a walk.

One week from the time they went for that first walk and overheard a conversation that changed a lot of lives.

"You sure you want to?" Bonnie asked, smiling at her husband. "You remember what happened last time we did that?"

"Sex?" he asked. "I remember sex on warm grass under bright stars."

She took his hand. "I think there's a rock out there with our name on it."

They strolled silently along the dark path.

She forced herself to not think about the events of the week. It was almost impossible to do, but somehow she wanted to get back to that feeling of just walking in the dark, enjoying Craig's company, and thinking about making love.

He held her hand and every so often would squeeze it.

But he said nothing either.

Seemingly, much faster than the first time they had made the walk in the dark, they reached the big rock.

Bonnie pulled him off the path and out onto the grass of the fairway.

She let go of his hand, kicked her shoes off, and laid down, enjoying the feeling of the warm grass against her skin.

They were both numb and she knew it, but somehow they had to come back to what they had together, put the week behind them and start new again.

She watched as he stood over her, his shape outlined against the stars.

"What are you thinking?" she asked, her voice sounding louder than she had expected in the night.

"Just how beautiful you are," he said.

"Really?" she asked, smiling up at him.

"Really," he said.

"And nothing else?" she asked.

"Just that you have too many clothes on for such a warm night."

She laughed, raised her hips and slid her shorts down and off her legs.

"How's that?"

"Better," he said, still just standing over her.

She sat up slightly and pulled her top over her head.

"Better," he said again.

She unhooked her bra and took it off.

"Getting close," he said.

She slid her panties off her legs and tossed them away.

"Perfect," he said.

She stood and gave him a long, hard kiss, then pushed him down onto the ground. "Now who has too many clothes on?"

They went through the same routine until he was nude and lying under her spread feet.

"I love this view," he said, staring up at her.

"Things don't look so bad from here," she said.

They stayed like that for a moment, then slowly she eased down on top of him, letting him hold her, letting him make love to her.

Finally, things were again right in the world.

They were together and that was all that mattered.

~

Coming Next Month
Dead Hand: A Cold Poker Gang Mystery

Coming Next Issue in *Smith's Monthly*

DEAD HAND

A Cold Poker Gang Mystery

#1...October 2013

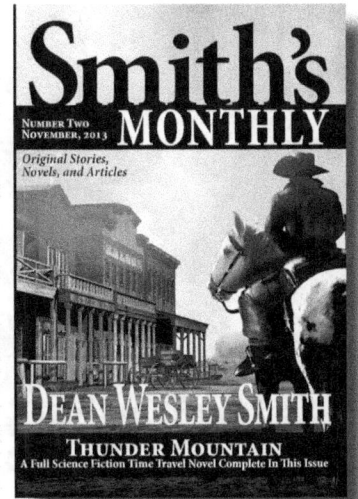

#2...November 2013

#3...December 2013

#4...January 2014

#5...February 2014

#6...March 2014

#7...April 2014

#8...May 2014

#9...June 2014

#10...July 2014

#11...August 2014

#12...September 2014

#13...October 2014

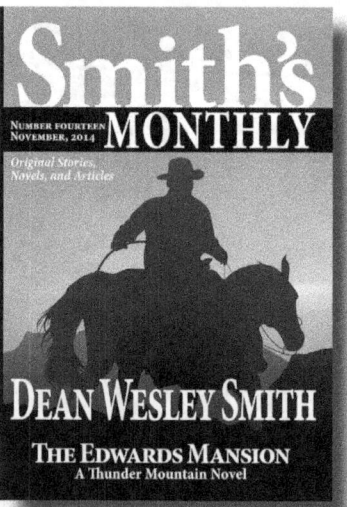

#14...November 2014

#15...December 2014

#16...January 2015

#17...February 2015

#18...March 2015

#19...April 2015

#20...May 2015

#21...June 2015

#22...July 2015

#23...August 2015

#24...September 2015

#25...October 2015

#26...November 2015

#27...December 2015

Thank You!!

I would like to thank the following wonderful people who support my blog and my work through Patreon. Your support is very important to me. Thanks!

Betsy Wilcox	Erick Lindman
Irette Y. Patterson	Christopher Ridge
Kathryn Rooney	Terry Mixon
Wendy Lee Maddox	James Husun
Jamie Curierre	Sherman Cox
Chris Cousino	Chong Go
Jane Lawson	Maria Grace
Shantnu Tiwari	Grondpom
Miguel Angel Alonso Pulido	Fen
Nancy Hendrickson	Robin Brande
Ryan M. Williams	J.R. Murdock
Jacob Proffitt	Kathleen McClure
Marian Goldeen	Gunnar Gunderson
Gary Speer	F.I. Goldhaber
Megan Bryce	Mary Jo Rabe
Michelle Tatam	John Kilgallon
Ann Tucker	Dave Hendrickson
Kari Wolfe	Jabberwocky
Albert Lemke	Eric Goebelbecker
Stacey Larson	Marsha Kessler
Diane Darcy	Scott Gordon
Krystle Jones	Martyn Folkes
Kari Gallagher	John
T. Thorn Coyle	Cj Lehi
Tasha Turner Lennhoff	Brenda Smith